THE COTTONWOOD STAGE

When their bank was robbed, the residents of Cedar Bluff did not wait for their town constable to pursue the outlaws, they did it themselves. Four of them, led by Fred Batson, set off on the trail. When they eventually managed to find the thieves, they thought their troubles were over. However, when the smoke settled, an army payroll was also recovered. What did it all mean and would the four men live to tell the final tale?

ROSS PADEN

THE
COTTONWOOD
STAGE

Complete and Unabridged

LINFORD
Leicester

First published in Great Britain in 1994 by
Robert Hale Limited
London

First Linford Edition
published November 1995
by arrangement with
Robert Hale Limited
London

The right of Ross Paden to be identified as
the author of this work has been asserted by
him in accordance with the
Copyright, Designs and Patents Act, 1988

British Library CIP Data

Paden, Ross
   The cottonwood stage.—Large print ed.—
Linford western library
I. Title II. Series
823.914 [F]

ISBN 0–7089–7766–9

Published by
F. A. Thorpe (Publishing) Ltd.
Anstey, Leicestershire

Set by Words & Graphics Ltd.
Anstey, Leicestershire
Printed and bound in Great Britain by
T. J. Press (Padstow) Ltd., Padstow, Cornwall

This book is printed on acid-free paper

1

Four Angry Riders

HANK LYTLE groaned inwardly with the coming of winter. Blacksmithing was undeniably hard work; not especially during the summer months. During summer the most uncomfortable work at best, was avoiding the dual nuisances of day-long heat and working forges which required cherry-red coals.

These were unavoidable chores, but if a slight breeze was blowing through the smithy, it brought relief.

Wintertime when the forge-fire was welcome, brought the part of his trade Hank had never liked. Shoeing horses in warm dry weather was what horseshoeing was all about, but shoeing in winter was different. It required knowledge of snow shoes, and as fate

1

would have it, rarely were two horses the same; it was impossible to lay by snow shoes. Each had to be particularly fabricated to individual animals. In summertime a blacksmith's slack time could be spent warping blanks into all regular sizes and storing them.

Hank had been a blacksmith for twelve years and he was not yet forty. He was about average height, powerfully muscled, was an even-tempered individual who had laughed more before his wife died than he had since.

She had been dead four years when the Citizen's Bank of Cedar Bluff was robbed. Smithing was hard manual labour; when his savings of six hundred dollars went with all the bank's cash Hank Lytle took it a lot harder than did other merchants, such as Alf Storey who owned the saloon and Jeffrey Towne who owned a big general store. Those were Cedar Bluffs two most lucrative businesses. Other losers, such as the harness maker, the rooming house proprietor and additional less lucrative businesses were hit hard. Their proprietors were up in arms.

Charley Prentice who owned the rooming house and whose wife was expecting their first child, told Hank Lytle that unless Constable Talbot ran the thieves down, he was going to round up as many townsmen as he could and do the job himself, no matter how long it took or how far ahead the outlaws were.

The robbery occurred minutes after opening time for the bank. By the time folks knew what had happened it was nearly mid-morning. When Charley Prentice talked to the blacksmith it was close to high noon.

Constable Talbot had left town shortly after breakfast riding south, loaded for bear and very upset. He'd lost two hundred dollars in the robbery.

By one o'clock Charley had four willing riders including Hank Lytle. The other two were a half-Mex who operated Cedar Bluffs only cafe, and the harness maker, who was older than any of the others, was tall, skinny, said little and almost always had a cud in his cheek. He was one of those lanky, sinewy Texans with shrewd notions and sound instincts. His name was Fred Batson.

The cafeman was lean, with black hair and eyes but fair skin. His name was Joe Angel — not really, his mother had named him Jésus, something both Joe and his father had refused to acknowledge and had always said Joe. Not Joseph just Joe. He was in his thirties and, like the Texan Fred Batson, had never been married.

The townsmen saw them off. Two, the blacksmith and the harness maker, did not own horses. The liveryman saw them off with trepidation; chasing outlaws was hard on horses, sometimes it was fatal, but he too had lost money in the robbery.

The thieves had taken the south stage road, as had Constable Talbot. There

4

was one thing which favoured the four horsemen, autumn was settling in, the hot days of summer were past, which made it easier on livestock. At least in that regard the liveryman could rest easy. What bothered him was that three of the riders were angry and eager, the fourth man, Fred Batson, was older; if anyone could prevail upon the novice manhunters to favour their animals, it would be Batson, who was riding a handsome young dappled grey.

The sun was beginning its long slide from the meridian, visibility was perfect. The day was warm but not hot. Nights this time of year were usually cold. It was a tad early for frost but guessing about things like frost — weather in general — was as pointless as peeing in a lake with an expectation of raising the water level.

Fred Batson did not take the lead but the younger men listened when he spoke, which was why they stopped at a way-station four miles from town and bought four bundles of food and four

5

canteens which they filled with water. Joe Angel and Charley Prentice rolled their eyes at this; there were creeks within a few miles in all directions, but they said nothing.

Fred rode close to the easterly berm watching for shod-horse sign where riders had recently left the main thoroughfare; Hank Lytle rode close to the opposite edge of the road. But neither saw the sign they expected to see. As for the roadbed, it had waggon tracks, stagecoach wheel sign, along with an assortment of saddlehorse tracks. They ignored all sign except that going south, but that wasn't especially helpful, lot of folks had ridden south. Fred tried to pick out distinguishing marks, as did the blacksmith, but here again, while there were spreader shoes and some with off-sets to correct pigeon-toedness, there was no consistency.

Charley's anxiety over losing his savings had kept him angry and vengeful until mid-afternoon when the riding became a slow process of watching tracks and saying little. He lost enough of his ardour to begin worrying about his pregnant wife.

He didn't mention this but when they had the rooftop of the way-station mid-way between Cedar Bluff and Cottonwood in sight, he wondered aloud whether they might not be on a wild goose chase.

Cottonwood was not quite as large as Cedar Bluff; it had started out years earlier as a simple way-station for the stage company. At that time there had been one long, low adobe building. It was still there and was still a way-station, but the town had grown considerably southward in a wide valley between two hump-backed, timbered mountains.

Fred led the way to the way-station where a bear-built man with a black beard and unruly black hair shot through with grey, met them out front. Fred explained who they were and why they were this far from town.

The massively bearded man shook his head. "If they'd went south on the road I'd have seen 'em. I start the chores at sunrise. Only thing I seen pass was a freight rig going north and a couple of rangemen who work for a ranch down here. I know 'em both."

Fred led the way; they cared for their animals, entered the main building for an early supper, and Charley asked the station-keeper how well he knew those cowboys he had mentioned.

His answer was succinct. "One's my brother-in-law. T'other one's a rangeboss named O'Malley. If you're wonderin' that maybe they robbed . . ."

Fred interrupted around a mouthful of food. "There was three outlaws, mister. There was three sets of horse shoes from in front of the bank to the lower end of town. The only thing that seems likely is that they used the southerly road. That's all. Three not two."

The station-master waited until an

expressionless Indian woman had re-filled their coffee cups and departed before he spoke. "They're clever if they been at their trade any length of time. They could have double-backed. Years back I run a general store. One morning, really early two fellers came with drawn guns . . ."

The Indian woman interrupted from a doorway. None of the men from Cedar Bluff understood what she said but the bear-built man did. He nodded and arose. He answered her in the same guttural language, then reverted to English to say, "'Scuse me, gents, the evenin' stage out back is ready to leave."

He left the room. Hank Lytle put down his eating utensils. "What evening stage? There hasn't been an evening stage sent out of Cottonwood in a couple of years. Only day coaches."

Joe Angel commented without looking up from his platter. "It could be a special hire," he said, and stopped further speculation until lanky

Fred Batson arose, ambled outside and down the side of the long building where there were corrals and sheds.

A Mexican hostler saw him, muttered something and the station-master turned, saw Fred and shook his head as he spoke. "Danged independents. Usually I don't service 'em but this one's a bullion coach. Gov'ment business so I got no choice."

Two men with exposed weapons, one with a shotgun the other man with a Winchester rifle, were standing back where the stage was being aligned for the hitch of four horses. They did not take their eyes off Fred. The man with smoke-tanned gauntlets, the badge of his profession, was obviously the whip. The other man, ruddy-complected with cold, pale eyes, with the rifle in the crook of one arm was just as obviously the gun-guard.

Fred nodded indifferent acceptance of this as he said, "We're ready to leave," and reached in a pocket. "You

10

wasn't around. We'd like to pay up an' be on our way."

The station-master approached Fred smiling. Fred handed him some silver, they smiled, nodded, and Fred went back around front.

Inside, his companions were finishing up. He jerked his head. "Let's move along."

They went out front, snugged up, mounted and rode at a dead-walk for several hundred yards southward until they were obscured by trees, then Fred boosted his horse into a lope and gestured for the others to do the same. They loped, but all three of them were watching Batson. He found a suitable place, veered abruptly off the road into some underbrush among a thick stand of timber, swung off and told the others to tie up and fetch their saddleguns.

He did not explain until they were concealed within a few yards of the roadway where he leaned looking northward. "Whiskers told me back there the stage they're rigging out is a

11

government stage carryin' bullion." He leaned back after seeing a stage raising dust in the northward distance.

Hank Lytle looked puzzled. "You want us to waylay a stage carryin' federal money?"

"No. First off, that's one of those old Cottonwood stages. The Cottonwood Stage Company went broke and left the country years back. An' the reason they went broke was because they got caught robbin' their own stages."

Joe Angel was scowling. "What's that got to do with this stage? Hell, they most likely sold off their rigs, Fred."

"It's not so much the stage," Batson replied, leaning to look northward again. "It's the harness. I never made harness for the Cottonwood Stage Company. The harness on them horses I made a couple of years back for a feller named Gus Hawkin."

Joe still frowned. "What about it?"

"Gus Hawkin had two sons. They both drove stage for the Cottonwood Stage Company. Neither one of them

12

was sent to prison when old Gus was. Batson paused to look at his companions. "There was two fellers out back where the coach was being readied. I never knew 'em but I saw 'em with Gus a few times. That's the two fellers I saw where the stage was bein' got ready. One's the gun-guard, his brother's the whip." Fred considered the faces turned in his direction. "You know why we didn't find where them outlaws left the road? Because they didn't leave it. They come arrer-straight to that way-station, shed their horses an' are now drivin' that old coach."

Joe, Hank and Charley did not dispute any of this but neither did they look confident Fred Batson wasn't jumping to a conclusion that wasn't exactly convincing. Eventually Charley Prentice asked a question.

"An' suppose we stop that stage an' it really is carrying government money? Suppose them fellers put up a fight an' someone gets killed?"

Fred was watching the northward

road intently. "The Hawkins wasn't everyday renegades. They was clever — an' they was coachmen. Not just saddle horse outlaws, they used stages."

Fred looked around at his companions who looked back without enthusiasm. They too could now see the stage coming toward them. Fred slackened his tense stand a little as he spoke again without taking his eyes off the oncoming rig. "I can't do it alone. If you boys want to let the coach pass, why then I'll just have to go along with you. But I'll tell you this — if it don't have the bank money from Cedar Bluff, I'll go back, you fellers can continue the search, and good luck to you."

Joe Angel was about half ready to be convinced. What he did not like was the idea of the four of them stepping out to block the road, with two heavily armed and probably resolute men sitting on the high-seat behind the horses where they could see Joe and his friends in front as exposed as crows on a fence.

Fred stepped back and turned. "I

could be wrong; them Hawkin boys could be makin' a legitimate money-haul for the gov'ment, but if they are, then whoever hired 'em needs to have his head examined. They got reputations that go back a long way."

Hank was watching the coach when he said, "It's not makin' a mistake that bothers me. It's maybe gettin' killed for no better reason than because you was wrong."

Fred threw up his arms in a gesture of exasperation and would have pushed past his companions to reach his horse if Joe Angel hadn't abruptly said, "Look!"

The Cottonwood stage had been halted down to a walk, the animals plodded along with loose lines. The two men on the box had opened a wrapped package and were admiring its contents. One man picked up something from the package on the seat between him and his companion, and held aloft a massive gold watch suspended from a thick gold chain.

The man holding the watch laughed. The sound carried easily to the ambushers in their tree-shaded flourishing undergrowth. What he said did not carry at all as the other man on the box took the watch, examined it closely, then handed it back as he made what must have been a disagreeable remark because his companion dropped the watch and chain into a coat pocket and leaned forward without another word.

Charley Prentice tugged Hank's shirt. "You get a good look at that watch? It belongs to old Henry May the banker. I've seen that thing a hundred times."

Hank caught Fred Batson's attention. "All right. You did a good job of guessin'. An' now what do we do? I never stopped a stage before."

Batson did not say whether he had or hadn't. What he did say was that it would have been better if two of them had been across the road, but since they weren't they should hide while Fred walked out into the middle of the road.

They did not have much time for discussion, the Cottonwood stage was almost parallel with where they were crouching.

Fred made one soft-said comment. "I remember that harness like I made it yestiddy." He paused.

"From what I heard years back the Hawkin boys don't just throw down their guns." He paused again, gauging the distance before also saying, "Stay out of sight. When the stage stops they'll be lookin' at me. I'm goin' to tell 'em to get down. When I say that — just in case they figure it's just me — you gents cock your weapons. Don't shoot, just cock 'em." Fred was arising in the underbrush when he said, "I know that'd work with me. I hope real hard it works with them . . . Remember; just cock the guns so's they'll hear 'em."

2

A Surprise

THE stage was one of those vehicles which despite its age, had been properly cared for. Each wheel tracked plumb straight and while aged stages usually rattled this one hardly rattled at all.

It was faded though, intimating whoever cared for it wasn't interested in appearance, the paint was faded where the name Cottonwood Stage Company had once shown clearly on each door.

Hank, Joe and Charley crouched, thumbs on gnarled gun-hammers, as the tall, skinny Texan emerged from the roadside cover and raised his right hand, palm forward, the same side on which he wore his leathered Colt. He wanted the coach to stop because its whip thought the man in the middle of the road was someone in need of help. A highwayman would have used a gun, the harness maker was standing out there alone looking helpless.

The whip hauled in on his lines and raised a booted foot to the binder handle. As the coach slowed then halted the gun-guard called ahead in an unpleasant voice. "Get the hell out'n the middle of the road." He jockeyed his rifle to bear on Fred Batson.

That was the moment three guns were cocked from the left side of the road, small intervals between the time each hammer was hauled back.

The gun-guard froze. His rifle was still pointing in Fred Batson's direction but he made no move to cock it. The man beside him, holding slack lines, seemed to have been turned to stone.

Batson did not draw his six-gun as he said, "Climb down. Driver, set the binders, loop the lines an' get down — on the near side. Follow your friend down on the near side, an' be real careful."

19

Both men climbed down on the same side of the road where the hidden men had cocked their weapons. As the gun-guard reached the ground without his rifle, he glared at Batson. "We're haulin' gov'ment cargo, you rob this coach an' the whole damned army'll be on your trail."

The skinny tall Texan did not act impressed. "Move closer to the brush — and drop them pistols."

He was obeyed. Hank, Joe and Charley stood up with their cocked guns. The whip and gun-guard looked from them back to Fred Batson. The gun-guard growled his threat again. "The army'll be all over you fellers like a rash."

Hank, Joe and Charley came out into the roadway. The whip gasped. "Hell, that's the feller's got the cafe in Cedar Bluff."

Being recognised was something Joe Angel probably anticipated. His was the only eatery for miles, every hungry individual in the country or passing through it had eaten at his cafe at one time or another.

Both the coachmen stood silently wary after the whip had recognised the cafeman. Hank and Charley went over to the stage, rummaged through the boot then inside the vehicle. Charley grunted. He was inside bending far over as he handed something out to Hank. It was one of those bullion boxes in common use. It had steel reinforced corners, a steel hasp and a big brass padlock. It was heavy. Hank put it on the ground.

Fred, still facing the coachmen with his cocked Colt, looked past them as he said, "Open it," to Hank and Charley.

The reason they hesitated was because of the lettering on the lid: 'United States Property'.

Charley said, "Which of them has the key?"

Fred looked at the gun-guard. "Empty your pockets." There was a large brass key among the items the gun-guard

21

dropped on the ground. He and the whip were watching Batson. He said, "Joe, give 'em the key," and faintly smiled at the coachmen.

The lid came up; Charley, Hank and Joe stood like stones. One of them finally found his voice. "Fred . . . This ain't our money. It's packets with paper round them that say 'U.S. Mint, Denver, Colorado'."

The malevolent-eyed gun-guard made a deaths-head smile at the skinny tall Texan. "You boys are in trouble up to your butts."

Batson seemed troubled, which he had cause to be. He asked the gun-guard where he had got the franchise for transporting money for the government, and got back a perfectly reasonable reply.

"We submitted a bid to the Denver Mint. It was the lowest bid." The gun-guard shrugged as though nothing more needed explaining, which it didn't. Batson put his attention on the man with the smoke-tanned gauntlets.

"What's your name?" he asked.

The gun-guard spoke before his companion could. "Mister; if you steal that army payroll they'll be after you like the devil after a crippled saint . . . Put the box back inside, get out of the road, an' we'll never tell a soul."

Fred said, "You're the Hawkin brothers. Which one are you?"

The captives were stony-faced. The gun-guard spoke in a harsh voice. "Mister, names don't mean nothing. I'll tell you one more time — put the box back an' get out of the road, an' no one'll ever know. Next time you try to rob a stage, be damned sure what you're doing."

Hank, Joe and Charley were behind the coachmen looking past at Fred, who did not seem, in their eyes, to realise what he had done — and which they had been his accomplices in doing.

Batson was unrepentant. He finally told his companions to re-lock the box and put it back into the stage. They worked like men anxious to right a wrong until Fred also said, "Tie the horses in back. We'll take these gents and their coach back to Cedar Bluff."

Joe stared. "Fred . . . if we highjack their stage an take it all the way . . . "

"The watch an' chain, Joe. We'll take 'em back an' let Mister May identify the one who took his watch and chain."

Charley, Joe and Hank had forgotten about the watch and chain. Now, they remembered and moved to re-load the box. After that had been done Hank spoke aside to Joe. "We didn't rob the coach. We just stopped it for a spell. Anyway, if Mister May will identify his watch'n chain . . . "

For the first time the whip growled at his partner. "We're losin' too much time. They'll wonder what happened . . . What's your name?" the whip asked and Fred answered without delay. "Fred Batson. I own the saddle'n harness works in Cedar Bluff. I knew you gents by sight. That was back before your paw was sent away for robbin' his own stages."

The whip ignored all this to say what had been in his mind. "Mister Batson, this delay is likely to hurt our franchise. We're supposed to haul on schedule . . . Two hunnert dollars for lettin' us pass, an nothin'll ever be said."

Fred regarded the whip over a long moment of silence, then said. "That'd be fair enough — except that what you gents stole from the Cedar Bluff bank was a lot more'n that."

The gun-guard snarled. "You're crazy. We didn't rob no . . . "

The whip cut him off. "Five hunnert dollars cash in hand, Mister Batson."

Hank, Joe and Charley were back there looking nonplussed. Their earlier suspicion that Fred had made a mistake and had involved them in it, began to fade.

When Batson stood silent the whip said. "Well. We can't stand around here for long; we're already maybe quarter of an hour behind. Five hundred cash and not a word ever said."

Fred had lost several hundred dollars when the bank had been robbed. He had no idea how much others had lost but he guessed it was in total maybe two thousand dollars, maybe even more.

But that occupied him only briefly. The five hundred dollar offer to let the stage go on its way was something he'd never heard of before. Coaches were robbed, they were not ransomed, or if they were he had never heard of it.

He didn't accept nor decline the offer, he asked the captives where the third man was who had been in on the Cedar Bluff robbery, and got a profane reply from the gun-guard. "You damned fool . . . You're crazy, mister, do you know that? You just been made a fair offer. Let's stick to what's important. An' we never raided no bank."

Fred didn't change expression. "You're the sons of Gus Hawkin. He went to prison six, seven years back, an' unless he broke out, he didn't help you rob the bank which was raided by three men . . . Who was with you an' where is he?"

The men from Cedar Bluff got a chilling reply to Fred's question from the west side of the road where they had hidden to stop the stage. All four of them recognised the voice; it belonged to that bear-built man from the way-station. The man who spoke some Indian dialect and had more hair on his face than a tame ape.

He wasn't alone, there was a lean, slight Mexican and two other men, large and grim holding cocked guns. The surprise had been so complete, the relief so great for the captives that the gun-guard exultantly exclaimed, "Right there on your left, Mister Batson. He was the third man. Now you boys shed your weapons an' line up alongside the stage."

The gun-guard made a grating laugh, "You damned fool, you could have made five hunnert dollars. Now you get nothin' but maybe a hole in the ground. *Drop them guns!*"

Batson dropped his gun. He was expressionless as he studied their captors. The bearded way-station boss was someone a person would remember a long time. The Mexican was lithe and young, was not noteworthy, and the third man Batson had seen in the corrals out behind the way-station, but only fleetingly.

As Charley, Joe and Hank followed his example and dropped their guns Batson looked steadily at the bear-built man as he said, "My name's Batson. Fred Batson. I'm curious mister . . . ?"

The bearded man growled. "Names ain't important."

"I'm curious about how you gents happened to be here."

The bear-like man growled his answer. "Just shut up. All of you pull up your pants legs."

They obeyed, none carried hide-out weapons. The whip and gun-guard spoke to the bearded man. "That tall scrawny one knows us. I got no idea

28

from where, but he even knew paw's in prison."

The bearded man studied his prisoners one at a time, before he addressed Fred Batson again. "Walk single file back where you left your horses. I'll be behind, these gents'll be on both sides. Don't even sneeze an' keep your hands where we can see 'em." He raised his voice in the direction of the gun-guard and whip. "Put the box back inside and get on your way."

They all waited until the men on the high-seat were ready, then the way-station boss called to them. "Tell Arnie what happened."

The whip talked up his hitch, the old stagecoach lurched and swayed, scuffed dust and gained speed as the bearded man addressed his prisoners.

"Now, lads, we're goin' back to the station. You'll ride beside one of us, an' if you get clever we'll kill you. Now — walk to your horses."

Charley Prentice obeyed every word to the letter. Joe and Hank did too.

All three were interested in the bearded man and what would await them at the way-station.

It did not require much time for them to find out. The ride was made slowly, the sun wasting away when they arrived behind the log station where they were ordered out of their saddles while the lithe Mexican went over and grunted up a pair of slanting doors.

It was a root cellar, in hurricane country they were called storm cellars. The walls were straight up and down of solid earth. The room was about twenty feet by twenty feet, had musty air, no light, and just before lowering the outside doors, the bearded man said, "I'm Ezekiel Bear. You just settle down and someone'll see you don't starve."

Someone ran a chain through both hasps of the slanting doors, placed a lock between chain-ends and loudly snapped it closed.

It was darker than the inside of a boot. The men from Cedar Bluff explored the walls by hand. Joe Angel said, "It won't get hot down here."

Hank's reply was waspish. "Is that supposed to make us feel better?"

When they were sitting against the vertical dirt wall Fred pondered aloud. "How did they happen to be down there?" No one had an answer. Someone lighted a match to fire up a smoke and for scant seconds they and their earthen jail were illuminated.

Joe spoke again, after a silence of about fifteen minutes. "We lost the damned money."

Fred spoke again, slowly and thoughtfully. Right now the money interested him less than other things. He said, "Was there a lot of money in that box, Joe?"

"Full," replied the cafeman. "I never seen so much money in my life. How about you, Hank?"

"Nope, I never did."

The harness maker persisted. "Would you say more'n was stole from the bank?"

31

None of them knew how much had actually been taken in the robbery but the men who had seen inside that box knew one thing for a damned fact. There had been a lot more money in that box than the Cedar Bluff bank was likely to ever have at one time.

Joe replied to the harness maker's question. "I'll make a guess, them bundles was neat and had a paper around each bundle. The lettering on them wrappers said United States Mint, Denver, Colorado. Them bundles was stacked in there one atop the other right up to the lid. Want me to guess? Maybe twelve, fifteen thousand dollars." Normally, such a figure would have brought derisive whoops. Not this time, not after Hank put in his two bits worth by saying, "Joe, them was fifty an' hunnert dollar bills." He sounded reproachful. "My guess is that it'd be a lot more than fifteen thousand dollars."

Not another word was said for a long time, not until Hank went forward to push on the slanting doors. They creaked but otherwise did not move. He hadn't really expected them to. But the doors were old, the wood had shrunk. There was a crack between them which allowed only a sliver of light to come inside. Hank hunched left and right using one eye to see out.

Behind him Fred was still pondering those wrappers of greenbacks. He eventually said, "There's somethin' goin' on. My guess is that the Cedar Bluff bank was only a small part of it. But I'll be damned if I can figure out where they got that much money . . . in this country. Hell, lump all the cowmen together an' the merchants in town an' you'd have to strain to get that much cash together."

Hank returned to his seat in back-wall darkness. It did not take the four of them long to reach a conclusion. As Fred had mentioned earlier, there was something going on, and it was not only big, it most likely was well organised.

Someone, they decided, was systematically robbing the countryside, and maybe a lot of other countrysides as well.

They were puzzling over the implications, particularly the fact that none of them had heard of any robberies, when someone rattled the chain, removed the lock and hoisted one of the cellar doors. It was the stone-faced Indian woman. Behind her back-grounded by sunlight, was the way-station hostler who hadn't said two words on the ride back from the failed stagecoach robbery.

Neither he nor the woman said a word. He stood back there watching, his right hand lightly resting on the butt of a holstered Colt.

By the time their eyes had become accustomed to sunlight the woman had placed four bowls on the ground and had retreated up the stairs, out of the cellar, and was turning to help lower and relock the door.

Joe dryly said, "Old whiskers is the

only one who seems to own a tongue."

The gruel was some kind of pounded corn and something else which had been cooked in oil, and except for chilli bits cooked into it would have been tasteless.

They ate without a word of complaint. Hours later when the same duo came for the bowls, Joe Angel tried to engage the Indian woman in a conversation using Spanish. That she understood they all recognised from the way she quickly raised her eyes to Joe, but did not respond, and departed as she'd done earlier.

Fred had been pondering again. As soon as they were in darkness he said, "If all the money came from our territory we'd have heard of it. So would other folks. That many thousands of dollars bein' stole would have raised a howl they could hear down in Albuquerque."

Someone rolled and lighted a smoke. Again, there was a fleeting smidgen of bright light. After it died Charley took up where Fred had left off. "Money in paper wrappers comes from a mint. Denver's the nearest one an' it's a hell of a distance from Cedar Bluff . . . Maybe it was an army payroll; maybe it was goin' to some big-town bank down south."

Fred was silent until he had a cud tucked neatly into his cheek. He spat once then spoke. "We got to get out of here an' find where the Cottonwood stage went."

Joe Angel spoke tartly. "How? A man'd have to have teeth like a gopher to get out of here."

Charley offered a proposal. "The next time the woman comes down here, we grab her, offer to let her go only if Whiskers turns us loose."

Fred was wagging his head from side to side but in total darkness the others did not know this, not even after he said, "Gents, my guess is that Mister Bear . . . that name sure fits don't it? . . . would tell us to go to hell. From the way he talked to her inside, the way he looked at her, I doubt that he'd care if we slit her throat."

"How about the feller who comes with her?" someone asked in the dark.

Batson shook his head again. "He don't come inside. It's too far to rush him from in here, up them little stairs where he stands."

Nothing more was said.

3

Cellar Doors

THE stone-faced Indian woman returned accompanied by the lithe Mexican. She brought bowls of the same gruel with peppers in it, he brought a bucket of water and a dipper.

The prisoners did not speak and neither did the lithe Mexican or the woman.

Charley Prentice drank his fill then asked how long this was going to last; he'd figured on riding out and returning. He had left a pregnant wife in Cedar Bluff.

No one could answer Prentice's question. He probably hadn't expected an answer, he was venting his exasperation and anxiety.

They knew it was dark out because

Hank peered through the gap between the doors and had seen stars in a blue-black setting.

They restlessly prowled their prison, groping, testing, swearing now and then. Only Joe Angel persisted in trying to get the warped old slanting doors open. One of them anyway. He had no luck. He turned away and swore.

Outside a man laughed.

There was a guard beyond those old doors. It was probably just as well that Joe hadn't gotten the doors open.

They came together again around the water bucket. When they spoke it could have been disembodied spirits. Each could hear the others but could not see them.

They were aware that if the guard was interested he could get down to that crack in the door, so they spoke in whispers.

Hank in particular, could be barely heard among the others when he said, "Them doors is hinged from the outside. The bolts come through the wood and got nuts on 'em."

No one spoke, they listened as Hank told them the rest of it. "Them bolts and nuts is rusted hard otherwise we could remove the nuts."

Charley waspishly said, "You got an idea, or are you tellin' us what we already know to make time pass?"

Hank ignored both the voice and the innuendo. He spoke again so softly that the others had to crowd closer. "Them old doors is weatherin' away." Hank held up a closed fist which the others could not see. He said, "I whittled one of the bolts plumb loose. Whittled all around it. It's still through the hasp out front but it's hangin' loose down here."

Hank said no more, he stood waiting, and as though on cue, the tall man asked a question to which he got a quick answer.

"The wood's about half rotten. Around the bolts it's punky enough so's a person can whittle it away, all around. I whittled around one bolt. It's

40

still bolted but both the bolt and the burr are floppin' loose." Hank stood there awaiting the judgment of the others. The lean, tall Texan said, "Are you certain?"

"It worked for me. If you got a better idea . . . "

Clearly not only did the speaker not have a better idea but after listening to Hank, the others were lost in thought. Fred Batson went over with both hands out front like a blind person seeking the doors. They could hear him groping until he found the hole with the rusty bolt and burr hanging loose of wood.

He did not return to the others, he clicked open his clasp knife and went to work. Not a word was said. They all went over to begin gouging half rotted wood around old rusty bolts.

Once someone's knife blade scraped across a bolt and the others hissed for silence. If that guard was still out there, and they had to assume he was, discovery would doom them.

As luck would have it the bolt Joe Angel was gouging had a hardened knot where the bolt-hole had probably been drilled through when the wood had been green. Now, that pitch had set-up like cement.

Joe swore under his breath, changed blades and made very little progress. They worked for an hour, rested and went back to work. Joe was sweating so much his hands were slippery. This did not improve his mood. He would wipe both palms and go back to whittling.

The others had their bolts hanging in holes where there was no wood. Joe swore until the others went over to help. They got barely any sawdust for half an hour. They did not give up. When one man stepped clear another one took his place. They eventually freed all the wood around the bolt.

They sat down in darkness with aching arms, hands and shoulders. Fred arose to peek out for the guard. He saw no one but his field of view through the crack was limited. He returned to the others. "I don't know if he's out there."

Joe was in a foul mood. "He'll be out there."

They sat in stony silence for a long time, until their cellar was beginning to fill with night-chilled air. They had a way to escape — lift away the door which was no longer bolted — and if that guard was there he could pick them off as they scrambled out of their dark place like tin cans on a rock. Hank went over to the door, very gently raised one corner a couple of inches and peeked out.

The others watched. Joe Angel was the least hopeful. Hank eased the door back down and returned to where the others sat. "He's out there, asleep sittin' on the ground."

No one even suggested trying to lift the door without arousing the guard. If it had been a regular door they might have tried, but this particular door was one of a pair, each half at least seven feet tall and four feet across. Fifty men could not have moved it without the chain rattling if they tried to lean it aside or prop it up so they could lizard-crawl out of the cellar.

Their latest problem was one of restless exasperation. They could escape from the cellar, but there was the other obstacle, the sleeping man out there with a gun.

Joe Angel was the slightest, most wiry of them. He made a suggestion that was a little better than continuing to sit in the cellar until someone came along and discovered what they had done.

He whispered. "The three of you can hoist the low end of the door. Not high enough to make the chain rattle, just high enough for me to belly-crawl out." He paused. The others were staring at him, something which was not quite discernible as he spoke again. "No more'n eight, ten inches, an' hold it until I'm out — then don't let it down, just hold the damned thing. If you let it down it'll creak or the chain will rattle."

They didn't ask the cafeman what he would do when he got out, they simply arose, approached the door, got into position and began to very slowly lift. If the door creaked — what the hell, all old wood creaked when the weather changed, it was the chain holding the pair of doors they worried about.

Three strong men — desperate men — had every reason to exert their combined strength with care. The door raised. They pushed upwards very gently, moving the old door scant inches at a time.

Joe left his hat behind, got flat down and sidled closer to the opening. When he was close enough and the gap was still not wide enough, the others took down deep breaths and with infinite care raised the door until Joe had his head out. He slithered like a snake. Within moments he was gone. They still held the door open.

They probably could have lowered the door as gently as they had raised it but Joe was their only hope, so they turned, braced the door open by leaning beneath it, using their backs instead of their arms and shoulders. They could stay in that position a lot longer.

To the bent-over men time crawled, less from their unnatural position which was awkward but otherwise not difficult, than because if this effort failed and later, along toward morning the woman and her companion appeared, found the door loose from its hinges . . .

Somewhere in the distance a dog barked twice, then was quiet. Closer, a corralled horse blew its nose. Joe heeded both sounds as he slipped down the side of the building where the guard was sleeping until he found what he needed — a stout length of dry wood. He slipped back, approached the guard from the left side and hit him once, hard. The man fell sideways.

Joe grabbed the man's six-gun, returned to the door, braced his legs, held the door from beneath, strained as he lifted and hissed.

"Climb out!"

It was ten degrees colder out of the cellar than it had been in it. They glanced at the sprawled man then went soundlessly to the pole corrals behind the way-station, sweated bullets for fear of discovery, found their saddles and bridles where someone had dumped them, led their horses out of the corral where other animals would have followed if Hank hadn't closed it before they could leave, saddled up and walked their horses southward; this was the hardest part, walking their horses.

Each one of them rode twisted looking back. No one yelled, no light appeared, no sound of horses being led up to be saddled. Joe finally was able to speak in his normal voice.

"Old Whiskers'll kill that feller who was supposed to be guardin' us."

Fred made a dry rejoinder to that. "Not if the feller comes to before the woman comes to feed us . . . If he's got a lick of sense he'll be long gone before Whiskers knows we got loose."

That certainly was a strong probability. Ezekiel Bear impressed folks as a man who would not like being made a fool of. And he wasn't.

They rode south. Not even Charley Prentice suggested they ride in any other direction. Somewhere ahead was that Cottonwood coach. Too far to be caught up to, but stages are large objects, people remembered seeing something as large as a stagecoach.

They had coats. All but Joe Angel had a hat. They bundled up and did not even slacken off until they had the Cottonwood settlement in sight, then they tied up in the alley behind the jailhouse. It was about time folks got out of bed. If the local lawman was an exception, they would have an even longer wait.

Maybe he was an exception. The first light was at the cafe where windows got blurry from the inside. They went over there, walked in, got a surprised look from the proprietor, a grizzled man with a bear-trap mouth, dark eyes and a fiercely upswept moustache. As they lowered themselves at the counter the cafeman said, "It'll be a while, gents. I just got the stove fired up."

He disappeared into his cooking area. Hank reversed himself on the bench to watch the front of the jailhouse. Eventually he turned back. The cafeman brought four platters and filled four coffee cups. He lingered as his first patrons of the day dived into their meals.

An old man shuffled in, exchanged greetings with the cafeman, shuffled to a far curve of the bench and was easing down as the cafeman set up a hot cup of black coffee. As the old man cupped both cold hands around the cup he said, "Did you see one of them coaches go south last night?"

The cafeman hadn't; he shook his head.

The old man drank coffee, which seemed to brighten him, put both cold hands around the cup again as he said,

"It was one of them coaches old Gus Hawkin used to run. Still had the letterin' on the doors." The old man drained his cup. The cafeman refilled it as the old man continued speaking. "I ain't seen one of them in years. Must be some stage company up north bought this'n. You'd think they'd paint over the name, wouldn't you?"

The cafeman thought so. "Seems likely. Did you know the driver?"

"Nope, didn't know the gun-guard neither, but they passed right along an' it was gettin' along toward dusk. Where you reckon it was going? Didn't have no passengers that I could see. It was makin' good time so I didn't get a chance to see much."

The cafeman looked thoughtful until the old man finished, then he said, "that'll spook folks, one of old Gus Hawkins coaches passin' through . . . You're dead right about one thing, Homer — nobody but a greenhorn would drive a Hawkin's stage without paintin' over the name."

Fred Batson caught the cafeman's attention. "Would that be the same stage company some feller who robbed his own stages some years back, owned?"

The cafeman had found some men who clearly hadn't heard the story of the Hawkin brood and what happened when they were caught robbing stages, including some they owned. He launched into a lengthy recitation with the old man farther down the counter occasionally nodding his head.

When the cafeman paused for breath the old man said, "I knew Gus well. I knew him back in Kansas, met him again when he came out here. We celebrated for two days." The old man ruminated while gazing into his empty cup. "Sad thing what happened to old Gus's wife right after he was sent to prison."

Fred was sympathetic. "It broke her spirit, her man bein' sent away?"

The old man's head came up. "Nothin' of the sort. She hung onto that rock field they called a ranch, took up with a feller by the name of Gruber, an' did the smartest thing she ever did. She run off her sons. They was born bad. She just upped an' told them never to come where she could see them again."

Fred agreed that ridding herself of worthless offspring was a good idea, and asked where, exactly, her ranch was. The old man, aided by the cafeman, spelled out directions in a manner even strangers to the Cottonwood country could not misunderstand.

The men from Cedar Bluff went out front where the air smelled of wood smoke. There were a few people abroad, but not many. The sun was still some hours away from creeping over the easterly rim of the world.

Fred had his first cud of the day. He spat once then said, "We better go visit Miz Hawkin."

Charley dissented. "We'll just be killin' more time an' as far's I'm concerned we already wasted too much time waitin' for the constable to show up."

The skinny Texan smiled indulgently at Charley. "Maybe she run 'em off, an' maybe she didn't, but one thing's a sure bet, bein' their mother she'd know a lot about her boys . . . Charley, we can't run that coach down. Hell, it was still daylight yestiddy when it went south after we stopped it. What we need, gents, is information about the Hawkin boys. Where they got friends, maybe wives an' families . . . Let's ride, gents."

Charley, Hank and Joe went with Fred to the horses, snugged up, got astride and let Fred take the lead.

He led them south of town about a mile where an old stump had been daubed red. At that point he turned to his left. The ruts were well worn. There were also old shod-horse sign, but to Fred it seemed a buggy was used more than saddle animals.

The old man had insisted the ranch they were seeking was three miles southeast of town. The cafeman had said it was closer to eight miles.

What mattered was that it would be at the end of the buggy-tyre road whether it was three, six or even ten miles.

They had eaten but they hadn't rested. A hot sun on a man's back makes him drowsy even if he's had a good night's rest. All but Hank Lytle dozed in their saddles. What eventually awakened them was a loud shout. It carried well, but in open country with clear air, sounds travelled farther than people thought.

They did not find whoever had shouted even though they watched the ruts and roundabout for fresh sign. In fact until they saw a set of ranch buildings with the sun slanting away, they did not see so much as a digger squirrel or a lizard, and the country they were traversing was perfect for those kinds of varmints.

What grass there was grew in clumps, like buffalo grass. There were trees but most of all there were rocks, mostly uniformly round and smooth. They were riding down into what had been a prehistoric lake. All those round rocks were grey, smooth, and scattered in all directions as though by a giant hand. Fred shook his head, among the men from Cedar Bluff he was the only one who had worked livestock ranges. Those round rocks about the size of a man's head were anathema. More good horses had broken their legs in this kind of country, and more men had got cracked skulls from being pitched against those rocks than folks could count.

Charley Prentice, who knew practically nothing about livestock and ranching, made a comment a man didn't have to be very smart to understand. "Why would anyone ranch in country like this?"

Fred smiled with slitted eyes studying the yonder buildings. "I can only think of two reasons, Charley. They inherited the place an' can't sell so they stayed.

Or maybe they didn't inherit it, but for a fact it's mighty poor grazing country — so I wonder why the old lady stayed out here. It's no place to make a living. It's no place for a woman to be, especially if she was alone."

They saw no signs of life although a dog barked. They did not see him for an excellent reason. He feared strangers, ran under the porch and did his barking from under there.

They were still some distance out riding abreast when a woman came out onto the porch, stood with both hands clasped under her apron watching them get closer to the yard.

Just once did she move, that was when she leaned and said something past the open door. After that she stood straight again, watching, both hands locked across her stomach under the apron.

A man appeared, but he went from behind the house without looking left or right, behind some outbuildings where none of the men from Cedar Bluff saw him again. Fred made a little clucking sound of disapproval without taking the slack out of his reins or giving any sign that he had seen that man rush for the bar where he could climb into the loft and flank the riders when they crossed toward the stiff-standing woman on the porch.

Fred only spoke once, that was when they reached the yard from the northwest. He quietly said, "Be careful, I got a big nose so's I can smell things an' right now my nose is tellin' me if we do anything that might fire up the old lady, her friend in the barn behind us just darned well might open up."

4

The Arroyo

THE woman was old, probably not as old as she looked, this kind of country was hell on horses and women. She also had a bitter droop to her mouth and steady, hard eyes.

When they halted out front without dismounting the skinny Texan, using the same unctuous tone of voice he'd used at the cafe, removed his hat and smiled as he said, "Good mornin', ma'am. My name's Batson. These here gents with me are real close friends . . . I knew Gus real well. We're trying to locate Wes an' Ambrose."

The woman's flinty expression deepened. "Is that so? Well, mister, I ain't seen hide nor hair of Wesley an' his brother in over a year."

Fred Batson showed an expression of disappointment. "We come a long way, ma'am. The boys told us where they lived so we thought we'd stop by."

The old woman's expression did not change. "I can't help you. I got no idea where they are." She paused before also saying, "An' I don't want to know. They're bad seed. Last time we met I told 'em both I never wanted to see either of 'em again. Them an' their paw ruint my life. I give 'em my best years. All I got back was meanness. I'm settin' out to make the best of the years I got left . . . what did you say your name was?"

"Batson. Fred Batson."

The old woman's grey gaze lingered on the skinny Texan for a moment before she said, "I can't help you, Mister Batson, an' if you find 'em, tell 'em what I said. I meant every damned word of it. Keep away from me. Don't even come onto my land."

The woman turned, entered the house and slammed the door. Charley looked disgusted. Fred shrugged and reined around to leave the yard. He got as far as the north side of the barn when a raffish, unshaved man whose suspenders were hanging on both sides as though in his haste he hadn't had time to hoist them where they belonged, hissed and beckoned.

The men from Cedar Bluff might have reined over there but Fred kept right on riding as he spoke from the side of his mouth. "Go north of the last buildings. We'll meet you up there."

Hank twisted to look back. There was a faint trace of a bitter-faced woman at the only front window. Hank sat forward eyeing Fred. He wagged his head. Fred was smarter than he seemed to be. When the four of them reined northwesterly beyond the yard they were hidden from view from the house. The unwashed, wet-eyed man had pulled up his braces. As they halted he approached Batson's stirrups as he said, "You boys lawmen?"

Fred shook his head.

The raffish man sniffled, looked around to be certain they could not be seen from the house and spoke again. "Is there a reward on her sons?"

Fred nodded. "I'm not sure how much, but it's plenty. Why? Do you know where they are?"

The raffish man got a sly look when he replied. "Well; I know about where they hide out. But there's got to be a reward. Them boys as soon shoot a man as spit. You understand?"

"And you want the bounty," stated Fred. "All right; but only half. Me'n my friends get the other half."

"Are you sure you ain't the law?"

Fred grimaced. "We got nothin' to do with the law. What's your name?"

"Harold Gruber. I live with the old lady. She's meaner'n a strikin' snake."

"Where are they, Mister Gruber?"

"I don't know they'll be there, but they come back there from time to time. Ride due west from that red-painted stump that marks the turn off to this place. Due west. There ain't no road. Due west about six, seven miles. You'll come onto a stump ranch. The old man who lives there is named Ned Parsons." Gruber paused to run a filthy cuff under his nose. "Remember — half to me."

Fred leaned down on his saddlehorn eyeing the raffish man. "If I'd been in your boots, Mister Gruber, before I got greedy about bounty money, I'd find out if we're friends of Wes an' his brother first."

Gruber blanched. The filthy cuff ran across beneath his nose again. "You ain't," he said in almost a whisper.

Fred straightened up, led the way in the direction of the red stump and did not look back. When they were miles from the yard he turned, looked at Hank, Joe and Charley, and burst out laughing. "That measly bastard won't sleep easy for a month . . . The old lady'll pump him. I like the idea he'll tell her we are friends of her sons. She could have told the truth, but if she didn't an' her boys are over at some stump ranch they won't be there when we ride in. I wouldn't trust that old bastard as far as I could throw him. His kind play both ends against the middle. Keep an eye peeled just in case he tries to ride around us to warn them we're comin'."

Joe and Charley exchanged a look behind the skinny Texan's back. Charley rolled his eyes heavenward; the three of them were learning things about the taciturn saddle and harness maker they had never suspected before. Fred was turning out to be a genuine asset. The way he talked at the Cottonwood cafe and now, he had sounded so sincere when he'd talked to the old woman in her yard . . . Hank rode up beside the skinny Texan with a question. "Fred, have you ever been an outlaw?"

It was the direct kind of question guaranteed to put nine men out of ten right up in the bit. For a moment as they rode stirrup the Texan was silent. He eventually turned his head and gazed coolly at Hank.

"No. You got any more personal questions?"

Hank dropped back red-faced and silent.

The land was marginally better than the area around the old woman's ranch. At least there were very few of those lake-bed round boulders, and the grass, which had been clearly over-grazed, was about eight inches tall.

Behind the harness maker Charley said something which seemed to have become uppermost in his mind. He told Joe and Hank they'd wasted half a day and before this fresh jaunt was over they would have wasted the whole day.

If Fred heard he gave no sign of it. He rode loose but erect in his saddle, studying the onward countryside. He abruptly halted about two miles from the road, rested both hands atop the saddlehorn and said nothing as his companions rode up and also halted. He did not have to say anything, the steel-rim tyre tracks were plain enough.

Fred raised his head looking northward as he said, "Well now, if I'm right, an' if we're lucky, what we got here is coach tracks." He jutted his jaw. "Come off the road somewhere back up yonder, maybe not too far from where he stopped 'em yestiddy." He gestured. "On a southerly angle but bearing more westerly from here on. You boys want to guess?"

Joe did. "Headin' for that ranch the saddle tramp back in the yard told us about." Joe looked up and around; as far as he could see in all directions the land was empty.

Charley suddenly said, "Hell; the coach's got to be ahead somewhere. That wouldn't be where anyone would send an army payroll, would it?"

Fred smiled, spat and sat briefly silent thinking. It was flat country where they were sitting. Except for a few trees at scattered intervals and some shallow erosion gullies. "We just might get our money back after all. But if we keep ridin' until we see a set of buildings, whoever's up there'll see us too."

They waited. Fred quirked around in his saddle, spat again and lifted his reins. "If they're up there, an' if they see us, an' if they run, it sure-lord won't be back north, it'll be southerly. At least I hope it is. I'd as soon they didn't go north. Mister Bear would tell 'em we're loose, if they don't already know it."

Joe nodded. "They could track us."

Fred nodded solemnly. "Let's go north a few miles, hunt up a place to set until nightfall." As he started moving he also said, "I hope Mister Bear ain't already out on that feller's ranch. If he is then they'll all know we're loose, and gents that'll make real impressive odds."

The three younger men rode in silence, watching on all sides. The skinny Texan occasionally also looked elsewhere but his main concern right now was finding a place where they could rest the animals, wait until sundown, and do both without being seen.

Shrewd individuals usually had someone just as shrewd doing some figuring.

They rode a fair distance with Batson always angling a little westerly so that when they made their ride in search of the ranch they would have cut off quite a bit of southerly distance.

It was good strategy, as was the idea of hiding until dark, the only trouble with it was that in this kind of country the only thing that got ignored was something that wasn't moving.

They were aiming for a stand of trees, not close-spaced as they would have liked, but near enough to make mingling shade.

Not until they were within handgun distance of the trees, no longer watching on all sides, did Charley jerk his horse to a halt and pointed.

A short distance northwest of the trees a man was sitting his horse like a stone watching them. When they halted, the man spun his horse and the earth seemed to have swallowed him where he must have ridden down into an arroyo.

Fred said, "Son of a bitch!" and hooked his startled mount into a run.

They sped past the trees and sure enough, there was a wide, deep gully with shod-horse tracks showing where the man had gone down there.

They hesitated on the brink. Hank said, "North." They slid their animals down the crumbly bank and boosted them over into a lope. Except for a piddling warm-water creek at the bottom, the arroyo was wide enough for the men to hasten forward. Where the creek bisected the bottom, Charley and Joe rode on one side of the creek, Joe and Fred rode on the other side. The tracks were so fresh dirt was still crumbling inward around their edges. But they already knew the man who had been watching them had only recently passed along.

The sun did not reach to the bottom

of the arroyo but it touched the upper part of the easterly rim, about a third of the way from the top.

Fred eased his mount out a full notch. The others sped along behind him. By their calculations the man they were pursuing could not be more than perhaps half to three-quarters of a mile ahead.

They were right. He was slightly more than three-quarters of a mile ahead sitting his horse staring alternately at a rainy-season mud slide which had blocked the northerly run of the arroyo, and his back trail. They saw him about as soon as he saw them. Both sides of the arroyo were straight up and down with no game trails. Ahead, was about an eight-foot mud slide. The man could only have escaped if he'd had wings.

He dismounted as the four Cedar Bluff riders dropped down to a walk, staring straight ahead. None of them made a move toward their holsters, the distance was too great for accuracy with a six-gun.

Neither did the bottled-up stranger. He swung to the ground, stood at the head of his mount watching those four riders approach. He was a thick shouldered man, not tall nor short. Hatbrim shade concealed his face until the men from Cedar Bluff were close enough to hail the man, which they did not do, but they all looked hard at his face. Not a one of them knew the man.

The stranger had long since considered the odds, which were very much against him. He considered each approaching rider, settled his attention on Fred Batson, the eldest, and when the four horsemen halted, he spoke without raising his face.

"You'll never get it done."

Fred leaned on his saddlehorn as he addressed the stranger, "Get what done?"

The stranger relaxed a little. "Find that stage coach."

Fred and his companions gazed at the stranger in long silence. Clearly, he

70

had somehow anticipated their arrival. Also, as frank as he had been there was no way to misinterpret his words. He knew what they were after, whether he knew them as individuals or not. Fred said, "You got a name?"

The reply was about what the men from Cedar Bluff could have expected.

"Yeah. John Smith."

"Mister Smith, how did you know we were coming?"

Again the man's candour was straightforward. "Did you ever hear of heliograph?"

That statement too, kept the four horsemen silent for a long moment. The only people who could have known they were coming over here were the old woman and the raffish individual who had sent them in this direction, the man named Gruber. Hank gently wagged his head. Whether they were on the right trail or not, and evidently they were, they were also in the midst of a nest of rattlesnakes.

Fred asked another question. "Who

sent you to watch for us?"

John Smith again answered candidly. "Old man Parsons. As soon as he seen the flash an' understood what it meant, he sent me to watch." The stranger's mouth pulled down slightly at the corners. "This damned mud slide wasn't here the last time I rode up this canyon."

Fred spat aside, squinted at John Smith as he said, "Well, I expect we'll have to take you to Mister Parsons' place with us. If he sees you comin' he'll figure things is normal."

John Smith gazed at Fred as though he thought he was dealing with an idiot. "When he sees me ride in with you four gents?"

"No. We'll go just so far. Just far enough for him to see you . . . Tell me, Mister Smith, which would be the best way to approach the Parsons place without bein' seen?"

The stranger's expression did not change, he seemed still to believe he was dealing with an idiot, but he was candid in answering the question.

"Mister, there ain't no way you four can get anywhere near without bein' seen."

Fred said, "After dark, Mister Smith?"

This time it was the stranger's turn to look surprised. "Maybe after dark."

"Which would be the best way — is there a barn between the main-house an' the yard?"

"Yes. If you come from the north."

Fred dismounted. His companions did the same. Wordlessly they knelt to hobble their animals, remove bridles and drape them from saddlehorns. The stranger watched all this without moving or speaking until Fred raised up gesturing. "Hobble him, Mister Smith. We got a few hours to kill. You wouldn't happen to be carryin' a pair of dice, would you?"

John Smith did not answer the question as he knelt to hobble his horse and remove the bridle, but when he stood up and was told to toss his six-gun away, while he moved to obey he shook his head at Batson. "I'll tell you how it is with me, mister. I work the old man's cattle. I know what else is goin' on but since he's never offered to let me in, I'm just his hired rider, an' that bein' the case I got damned little reason for riskin' my neck . . . When I don't come back before nightfall he's goin' to worry."

Hank had a question for the rangeman. "How many is at the ranch with Mister Parsons?"

"The Hawkin boys. As I was ridin' over this way I seen some dust from the north. Maybe he's got more company, I didn't wait around to see who made that dust or which way they were goin'."

Charley Prentice groaned. "From the north? Fred . . . ?"

Batson nodded. "Whiskers from the way-station." He smiled enigmatically at the younger man. "Now why would he ride hell for leather to this ranch? If I was in his boots, I'd be trackin' the four of us."

John Smith listened and said nothing. He knew his employer wanted these four to be watched. He'd been told to report back as soon as he saw them coming from the east side of the roadway. He had worked for old man Parsons for two years, in that length of time he had seen several strange things, and whatever his name really was, he was not a fool. He had been fitting bits and pieces together in his mind; he still did that as he listened to his captors. Without anything but suspicion to base his assumptions on, he was beginning to understand something that had happened the night before. He had been dead to the world in the Parsons bunkhouse when a large vehicle had come into the yard, and because the vehicle had arrived at a walk he might have slept through, but someone shouted and a horse whinnied.

It was a faded old stagecoach with lettering on the door, but it had been too dark to make out the words, and he had made no attempt to light a lamp or open the bunkhouse door. He was supposed to be sleeping. He watched out the small front window. Darkness impaired vision but he had seen two men climb down. He recognised them both from earlier visits to the yard. He knew their names but that was all he knew, and he might not have known that much if he hadn't heard old man Parsons call them by their names.

When he straightened up from hobbling his animal the skinny older man with the slight Texas accent told him to join the others for the long wait.

As they got comfortable that sun line on the easterly wall of the arroyo climbed steadily higher as the sun sank in the west, but at this time of year days were long. He went over where the men from Cedar Bluff were sprawling, eased down and declined Batson's offer of a plug. "Never could chew," he told him. "I tried twice an' got sicker'n a tanyard pup both times."

As they waited John Smith dug out the makings, rolled and lighted a smoke. Joe Angel, whose interest in the rangeman had been captured by the way John Smith answered every question frankly and honestly, said, "Mister Smith, who is old man Parsons?"

Smith trickled smoke and watched ash grow on his smoke before replying. "An old widower who runs three, four hundred mammy cows and a bull to every forty cows." Smith looked straight at Joe Angel. "That's all I know, friend . . . But I didn't come down in the last rain neither."

Fred had a question, and after he asked it none of the men from Cedar Bluff expected an honest answer; it was one of those questions folks did not ask. He said, "I been wonderin', Mister Smith. You hired on with an old man who has an isolated cow outfit, an' you use the name John Smith — well — I wasn't born yestiddy, so I wonder — only someone who needs to hide out for a while does them things. Am I right?"

John Smith did not reply. He gazed at Fred Batson with an expressionless face and changed the subject. "I don't recall whether there'll be a moon tonight or not, do you?"

5

Mexican Stand-Off

DUSK arrived down in the arroyo an hour before it settled over the countryside above. The men rigged out almost casually, they had time to kill. By the time they were ready to ride back southward and out of the arroyo it was getting dark in the arroyo and the diminished visibility which accompanied dusk up above was beginning to shade away into pre-night gloom.

John Smith did not speak as Fred led off westerly, but when Batson had gone far enough Smith said, "See them big rocks? Turn south from there."

That was all he said. Hank, Joe and Charley got the impression John Smith was having trouble with his conscience; that he did not much care for his employer he had made plain back in the arroyo but it was unwritten law that rangemen were loyal to the brand they rode for.

There was no talk as the light failed minutes at a time, until Fred asked John Smith about the yard ahead. It turned out to be like most other cow-outfit yards, there was a big barn, a smaller main-house, outbuildings to the east and west, with the yard between open and nothing to impede the view northward with only the main-house blocking some of the southward view.

Moonlight was late arriving and not especially spectacular. A dog barked otherwise the yard was quiet. There were lights at the main-house and what appeared to be an unnecessarily large bunkhouse. No other buildings showed light.

Smith said something short to Fred Batson, who halted, unloaded and stood at his horse's head, peering ahead. The other men also dismounted.

Fred hadn't said a word for the last mile or so. Now, all he said was, "Where will the Hawkin boys be — the main-house or the bunkhouse?"

John Smith replied dryly. He did not appear to have completely overcome his sense of duty even though, with no gun in his hip-holster and in the company of captors he did not know very well but had recognised as his kind of people, his sense of loyalty still bothered him to some extent. He said, "The old man'd have Ambrose and Wes at the main-house. That's how he's always treated 'em before." John Smith paused before adding a little more. "I'm the only rider the old man has an' as far as I know he wouldn't be havin' guests, so who's in the bunkhouse?"

None of the men from Cedar Bluff spoke.

The dog gave up his barking. All he knew to do was give warning that there were strangers out yonder. What his owner might do after that wasn't the dog's affair. He curled back up and dozed.

Joe said, "Fred, if we take the main-house without makin' a ruckus, we might be able to get them Hawkin boys an' be gone before whoever's in the bunkhouse knows we been here."

Fred nodded slowly without taking his eyes off the main-house. Joe's notion was identical to the idea he had been considering.

He did not particularly like the notion of there being men in the bunkhouse. If there was a ruckus at the main-house they would most likely come boiling out. Had Smith lied about being the only rider? He didn't think so. If he'd made a guess he might have acted differently. At the present time there were only the mother of the Hawkin boys and that double-crossing old bastard she lived with who knew where the men from Cedar Bluff might be.

Fred stood hip-shot trailing reins in his left hand as he watched the yard and pondered. There was a chance Ezekiel Bear from the way-station and his hirelings might have either been informed or maybe just suspected that the four riders from Cedar Bluff were over here.

The longer Fred stood pondering about this the more he was inclined to neutralise whoever was the bunkhouse first, then go over to the main-house. When he made his decision he said, "Charley, you'n Joe go around behind the bunkhouse. Hank, you'n me'll go to the front."

Charley said, "What about Smith?"

Before Batson could reply John Smith spoke. "Gents, I'm goin' to head north and keep on ridin'. I've had all of the old man and his shenanigans I want."

Although John Smith seemed and sounded sincere, the men from Cedar Bluff considered him without comment. There was a good chance John Smith would ride away, circle around and return. If the situation hadn't been critical Fred would have let him go.

But it was critical so he told John Smith to dismount. He took Hank with him into the big barn where they tied him hand and foot, gagged him with his own bandana and left him in a horse stall. When they returned Joe and Charley were waiting on the ground beside their horses.

Fred nodded at them. "Get behind the bunkhouse. Don't do anythin' or make noise unless you hear me or Hank call out. Maybe we can get inside an' catch whoever's in there without trouble . . . let's go."

They tied their animals north of the barn out of sight of the main-house and paired off. As Joe and Charley were making their surreptitious way down the backsides of the barn and other outbuildings Charley said, "I got a bad feeling, Joe. I got a hunch them men from the way-station is in there."

"The bunkhouse?"

"Yes."

Joe moved like an Indian, soundlessly and taking every advantage of the darkness. He had no comment to make about his partner's worry.

One of the interesting — and exasperating — things about Mother Nature was that she was absolutely indifferent to the machinations of men. Joe and Charley were between a three-sided big wood shed and the bunkhouse when the rear door opened, a man was briefly silhouetted until he closed the door, and if he hadn't moved Joe and Charley would have been able to discern him against the background of the bunkhouse and the darkness. But he did move, he went out a hundred or so feet from the bunkhouse, edged up to a bedraggled tree to pee, and as he did this he slowly gazed in all directions.

Joe and Charley could only crouch against the ground. There was no cover, they were between two buildings unable to move without being detected.

The man turned slowly back from the tree, paused to roll a smoke which he did not light for some reason, and gaze up at the sky then lower, still moving his head slowly before he struck out for the bunkhouse.

When the man was gone Joe leaned to whisper. "Do you know who that was?"

Charley nodded. "The Messican from the way station."

"You know what that means, Charley?"

"Sure, it means Whiskers and his friends are over here."

"One of us better go tell Fred an' Hank."

Charley put a restraining hand on his companion's arm. "Why? It don't make any difference if them three are in there; Fred knows someone's here. It don't much matter who — just that someone's here . . . Come along."

They got closer to the bunkhouse when suddenly the light inside was doused.

Charley and Joe were on the north side of the bunkhouse waiting and listening before they went around where the rear door was. Charley's premonition firmed up stronger than before. When Joe wanted to move into position Charley raised an arm to hold him where they were.

Bunkhouse doors were commonly opened and closed by a *tranca*, a length of wood that, on the inside, rested on a half-stirrup-like hanger. To open and close the door there was a short length of rope or leather attached to the hanger-side of the scantling which had a loose-fitting bolt on the far side. When the rope was pulled the *tranca* was raised.

This was the most common variety of door closure in areas where there was no access to regular door-hardware.

The night was still, even the smallest sounds travelled. Where Charley and Joe were pressing flat on the north side of the darkened bunkhouse the sound which reached them, although muted, was nonetheless softly audible. Someone had raised the *tranca* inside the bunkhouse.

Charley's premonition held him

motionless, barely breathing. The door swung inward slowly and almost without sound. Joe whispered. "Someone's comin' out."

Charley palmed his six-gun. If his premonition was correct it wouldn't be just one man emerging. He wanted to swear. That Mexican who had come out had seen them. Charley had to admire the Mexican's calm reaction. The only indication that he knew two men were crouching north of the bunkhouse was the fact that he had not lighted his cigarette.

Joe would have edged around to see if Charley hadn't raised his arm again, stiff as iron this time. Joe leaned back. There were three of them. Charley made this deduction from the soft, grating sounds of boots over gritty soil. It was the right number; Whiskers, the Mexican and the other way-station yardman.

He would have given a good horse to be able to go back the way they had come to warn Fred and Hank.

He could not move; he had heard their bootsteps and they would hear his.

Joe's anxiety had been increasing in leaps and bounds. He could not see around the corner of the bunkhouse, but he knew their enemies were out there. Right at this juncture he did not try to guess how they'd happened to come out. He watched Charley for his cue.

The utter quiet was interrupted out front by the sound of a brief scuffle which lasted only moments. Charley and Joe worried even more now. Joe was getting upset because Fred and Hank didn't brace the front of the bunkhouse. They would find it empty but whatever they did would provide a diversion and Joe did not like being pinned against the log wall at his back.

He would have worried even more if he had known that one of the night-stalkers behind the bunkhouse had slipped away in darkness heading for the main-house, where a light still burned.

Charley very slowly sank to the ground. Joe followed his example. They sweated, whoever had come out of the bunkhouse would be moving, prodding, hunting, shifting position often and they were unable to move. It was almost more than Joe could stand. Charley felt him squirming and reached, closed a fist around Joe's arm to warn him to be still. It worked.

The hush was suddenly broken by the sound of a door around front being violently kicked inward. Joe had his diversion and could not take advantage of it. Whoever was hunting them could have gotten northward by now. Any movement would bring gun-thunder.

Charley mopped sweat off, looked at his companion then had his attention caught by men making no effort to conceal themselves inside the empty bunkhouse. They tracked the movement by ear. When someone inside approached the rear door Charley and Joe held their breath. If Fred or Hank walked out there was a good chance they would be shot.

Someone did walk out and there was no gunshot. Joe pinched Charley's arm and jutted his jaw. A shadow was moving swiftly in the direction of the barn. Joe took a forearm rest and was cocking his gun when Charley stopped him. Charley did not believe that retreating, hastening silhouette would be Fred or Hank but he did not want to be wrong. He shook his head. Joe slowly eased the hammer down and scowled. At the same moment a man spoke distinctly from the rear of the bunkhouse. Not loudly, but distinctly.

"Charley? Joe?"

Without waiting Joe scrambled to his feet. Charley was more cautious but eventually he also got off the ground. Joe did not raise his voice when he said, "Hank? Fred?"

The four of them came together behind the bunkhouse. Joe explained what had happened. He did not mention the Mexican having detected them crouching between buildings. Right at this time it did not matter how it had happened that the men staying at the Parsons ranch had discovered that they had night-stalkers. What mattered was that they had made that discovery.

Charley mentioned the fleeing silhouette. He had scarcely finished his tale when a rider on a running horse left the yard riding northward like the wind.

Fred laconically said, "Well, that whittles down the odds by one." He asked where the other two were and when he got no reply, he addressed his companions in the same laconic manner. "So much for bein' clever. Odds are a million to one them other lads are over at the main-house by now."

They went up through the bunkhouse and saw a darkened main-house on their right. They went back to the bunkhouse table, sat, all except Joe who shook an old speckle-ware coffee pot, found it nearly empty and went to join his companions as Charley Prentice raised a foot to the table's bench and said, "I'd kind of like to get this over with, my wife's due to spring in another month."

The others did not have this problem, they were pondering a different dilemma when Fred said, "We only got one advantage — darkness."

Hank agreed. He also said, "It ain't gettin' over there that bothers me, it's the odds, an' the fact they're forted up in the house."

Fred returned to the doorway, chewed pensively as he eyed the main-house and did not face around when he said, "Six. I make it out to be maybe six over there."

Joe corrected that. "Five. One left out of here like the devil chasin' a crippled saint."

Fred turned with a shrug of bony shoulders. "Five then — and a damned stout log house to protect 'em." He gazed around. "We can likely get around behind the house."

Joe nodded. "An' then what?"

Fred did not know. "Just gettin' over there'll have to do for now."

Joe the cafeman did not look reassured and Hank and Charley were silent. Joe went prowling the dark bunkhouse. He returned with an old trapdoor Sharp's buffalo rifle. Charley looked bemused in the gloom. "What are you goin' to do with that thing — did you find any ammunition?"

Joe shook his head and put the old gun on the long bunkhouse table. "There's no slugs for it anyway," he said using a tone of voice of deep regret. He'd heard tales of the power of those old guns since childhood. He'd never had one in his hands before.

Fred returned to the doorway gazing southward. The house was dark and ominously silent. He got rid of his cud before turning back to say, "Let's see if we can get around in back."

They followed Fred. South of the bunkhouse there were two structures, one had three sides and a wide-open front facing the yard. It was for storing winter wood. They got past that building without incident. The gap between the wood shed and what appeared to be a storage house, was about sixty or seventy feet. Beyond that there was open ground for quite a distance. It had no cover of any kind, not even bushes or trees.

They lingered beside what Joe mistakenly thought was a smokehouse, which it could have been; the walls were at least two feet thick, chock full of sawdust. Actually, it was a cooler-house, where ranchers stored perishables.

Hank slipped to the southernmost corner, removed his hat and peeked out. They were close enough now to be able to make out details at the main-house. Hank hissed for the others to join him. A very important detail of the front veranda and long front wall was three rifle barrels clearly evident along the wall from the inside.

Fred make a clucking sound of disapproval. Charley drew back looking behind them and westerly. There was nothing to be seen, no movement, nothing threatening.

Joe, who had worried about both John Smith and the shadow they had seen running for the barn, worried about those two being behind them in the night. He also worried about something else.

"Suppose that feller who run off goes to round up some neighbours and comes back?"

No one answered. For one thing, on their ride out this far they had seen no other ranch-yards. For another thing, if what they had heard about the old screwt who owned this place, even if he had neighbours, his disposition being what it was, they might be glad he was in trouble.

Fred gauged the distance between the store-house and the west side of the house and wagged his head. Those guns did not encourage him. Hank came over to the doorway. "One man might make it," he said, "if the others shoot up the front of the house while he's runnin'."

Fred considered Hank. "An' how does the rest of us get over there? If they seen one feller try it they'll be waitin' for the rest of us."

Hank answered curtly. "I'll make the dash. One man around behind the house'd be better than standin' around here until sunrise."

Fred said no more. The others watched Hank head for the rear door. Joe gazed sadly at the old buffalo rifle. Three or four shots out of that gun would blow holes in the wall of the main-house.

Charley stopped Hank. "I'll go out back an' cover you from the corner of the bunkhouse."

They left the building together. Joe looked at Fred, who had a fresh cud in his cheek. By this time their eyes had become accustomed to poor light.

Fred jerked his head, unshipped his

97

belt-gun, returned to the open front door of the bunkhouse with Joe coming up beside him.

Fred spat and shook his head. "That's a hell of a long run," he said, more to himself than to his companion.

Hank and Charley got to the southwest corner of the log structure and paused briefly to peek around. Those three gun barrels were still visible. Charley raised his six-gun. "Hank, good luck. Zig-zag."

His companion nodded while studying the front of the dark main-house, took down a deep breath and launched himself forward in a crooked pattern.

The dog which had barked earlier either saw or scented the running man and barked furiously.

Charley raised his six-gun, gripped the wall with his freehand to make an arm-rest of aiming, ignored the dog and watched those three rifles with the hammer at full cock in his right hand.

6

A Night of Confusion

THERE was no gunshot. Charley, as tense as a wound spring, saw one rifle move slightly but did not turn where Hank had raced for cover. He waited but none of the guns fired. As he eased the hammer down and holstered his sidearm he looked for Hank and did not see him, which meant he had reached the west side of the house. Charley returned to the others frowning. He told them what had happened and Fred Batson said, "One of two things, lads, either they didn't see Hank or they ain't all there."

The last half of his remark caused uneasiness. Joe went to look out back. If there was anyone back there they were motionless; when he returned he closed the door at his back.

Batson was again leaning in the front doorway. "We wait," he said. "Now it's up to them — and Hank." Joe, who did not like waiting, sat down at the bunkhouse table. "Suppose they left the house by the back? They'll find Hank sure as hell."

Fred turned. "My guess is that if they left the house they done it maybe half an hour ago." He gazed steadily at the cafeman. "Things might be sort of reversed; we'll be forted up an' they'll be loose."

Charley paced restlessly but Joe remained at the old table. When the gunshot sounded all three of them jerked upright.

There was no second gunshot. "Sounded like behind the house," Joe said. All three of them knew what that could mean; Hank ran afoul of someone he — and his friends — had thought would be in the house.

Joe made an unusually prescient

remark. "It don't pay to underestimate folks, Fred."

Batson should have taken that as a rebuke but if he did he gave no indication of it. He spoke on an altogether different subject, almost as though he was not replying to Joe.

"Somewhere they got that Cottonwood stage hid. They won't have time to unload the money-box to split up the money among 'em before they run for it, and they won't try to run with the box, it'll be too heavy an' awkward . . . Gents, we got to find the stage."

Charley frowned in the gloom. "What about Hank?"

"You go look for him," Fred replied. "Me'n Joe'll hunt for the stage. It's got to be around, somethin' that big can't be hid very easy."

Charley disappeared out the back door. Joe stood gazing at the skinny tall Texan. "The barn?"

Fred's reply was in that laconic tone again. "Maybe, but if it is it's got to be hid real well. Let's go, Joe."

They left by the rear door, exactly as Charley had done. This was not Fred's favourite choice, if their enemies were somewhere outside the house they could easily be out in the night behind the bunkhouse, but evidently this was not the case because both Charley and Joe left by the rear door and nothing happened.

They were making a painstakingly slow way in the direction of the barn when the unseen dog sat back and furiously barked. This time he did not stop. Something over in the vicinity of the main-house had his full attention.

Joe looked over his shoulder but saw nothing. Fred was adept at utilising shadows and darkness. He re-traced his earlier path. There were times when Joe had to remain close or miss seeing the harness maker altogether. If he hadn't been so preoccupied he might have wondered how a man who worked with leather in a shop in town could be so good at this sort of thing.

They did not reach the barn. There

were two thunderous-loud gunshots from that direction, either inside the barn or very close to it.

Fred sank to the ground.

There were several horses in an old pole corral who had a fit when those shots sounded. They raced around and around inside their pen. It didn't take much to panic horses; gunshots in particular would do it.

A willowy silhouette appeared sidling toward them along the back of the barn. The man was intently watching the rear barn opening.

Fred jerked his head and moved eastward while simultaneously making some northward progress. His intention was clear to Joe, Fred wanted to be parallel to that silhouette on its right side when it left the barn-area and continued to slip southward where Fred and Joe were waiting.

The waiting men were abruptly rattled by a gunshot west of the barn farther out than they could imagine any reason for a gunshot.

Joe edged up closer to Fred as the silhouette abruptly dropped flat. They could make him out because they had been watching him, but it was more difficult to see him prone than it had been standing up.

Impatient Joe Angel leaned to whisper to the older man. "Maybe it's Hank or Charley."

Fred shook his head without looking away from the prone man. He did not say what he was thinking. It was not possible that either of their friends could have got this far south of the main-house or the bunkhouse. It baffled the skinny tall Texan. He was willing to believe the men from the house could have reached the barn; they'd probably had time to skirt around on the east side of the yard while the men from Cedar Bluff had been in the bunkhouse, but the longer Fred thought about it the more baffled he became.

Joe whispered again. "They got to fightin' among themselves," he whispered, and as before Fred did not reply. He was watching the man on the ground between himself and the barn. Whoever he was, he was beginning to squirm backwards.

Joe started to move. Fred caught hold and forced him to stop moving. The man who was awkwardly crab-crawling backwards was watching both the rear of the barn and westerly where that last gunshot had sounded.

Fred watched and waited. He eventually leaned close and whispered to Joe. "Stay still. If he don't get up an' run he's goin' to back right up to us."

They waited. The crawling man stopped moving. They could see him fairly well, at least his outline on the ground. He was, in fact, within easy six-gun range.

There was a long period of silence. Fred was convinced there was at least one man in the barn, maybe more than one, possibly the Hawkin brothers and Ned Parsons. What troubled him in a less-concerned way was that gunshot from several hundred yards west of the yard. By his count they still had five enemies, and where Fred and Joe were lying in the darkness, that made odds of nearly two to one. He did not count Charley or Hank for a good reason — wherever they were, they were not where Fred wished they had been — close enough to support Fred and Joe.

The crawling man began his backward slithering again, still watching the rear of the barn and the westerly country, out where the last gunshot had sounded.

He was less than a hundred feet from the two men waiting to grab him when he stopped crawling again, and this time Joe's impatience made him raise up slightly. Fred would have hit him if he dared. He turned, glared and pointed to the ground. Joe got flat down again. He was holding his six-gun pointing in the direction of the crawler. It was not cocked but that could be remedied in the blink of an eye.

Fred's irritability had been increasing by the minute. If Joe moved again the man they were watching would surely hear. He put a hand on Joe's arm and bore down with pressure.

The crawler twisted slightly as though to look backwards. Fred and Joe held their breath. The man made his survey and faced forward again. He had probably wanted to be sure he was not being flanked, but whatever his thoughts it was clear his particular worry was the barn.

He crawled again until he was almost within Fred's reach. The men from Cedar Bluff scarcely breathed. Joe very slowly holstered his six-gun.

The man raised up, supporting his body with both hands like a lizard. Fred could feel Joe tensing. The man was close enough, Fred also raised up. He only had to move a yard or so. At the moment Fred's six-gun was arching, the man turned. The blow which was supposed to hit his head, came down alongside it and ground into his shoulder. The pain was excruciating. The man let go of his six-gun to writhe in agony. Before he could yell Fred struck again. This time the blow landed squarely and the man went limp.

Fred waited to see if there would be any reaction from the barn-area. When there wasn't he and Joe grabbed the unconscious man by both ankles and dragged him back to the north side of the bunkhouse where they propped him up, removed his hat and squatted — looking at a complete stranger.

Fred let his breath out slowly. Joe stared as he softly said, "What'n hell — that's no Whiskers or his Messican, and it ain't the other hostler . . . Who the hell is he?"

There would be no way to identify the stranger until he regained consciousness which might not be very soon. They squatted in darkness staring until Fred finally spoke. "I think what we done, Joe, was figure wrong. It wasn't just Parsons and the Hawkin brothers in the house. If we guessed wrong an' this feller was also in there — then whoever he is, there's one hell of a good chance he wasn't alone. Where the hell are Hank and Charley? Joe, I'll tell you straight out, it looks to me like there's somethin' else goin' on, an' I don't like it."

Joe had no answers. He went over, plundered the pockets of the man with a goose-egg forming on his head, put what he'd found on the ground where Fred could see, and brushed aside a clasp-knife, some crumpled greenbacks, some silver coins and something else. They sat staring at it; a small rounded circlet with a star inside inscribed United States Marshal.

Joe made a clucking sound. Fred picked up the badge, turned it over several times then tossed it back among the stranger's other plundered possessions as he said, Joe, "I'm beginnin' to get an idea; that payroll money they stole . . . Why else would a federal marshal be sneakin' around out here?"

Joe was less interested in that enigma than he was in something else. He abruptly exclaimed: "That gunshot from west of the yard — there's more'n likely other lawmen or posse-riders out there . . . You remember the feller we heard leavin' the yard runnin' like a scairt rabbit? I'll lay you ten to one he was in the house an' when somethin' was done or said about government lawmen being out here he decided to run for it while he could."

Fred Batson did not comment, he arose and, with Joe following, went along the rear of the bunkhouse to the corner where Charley had watched Hank make his dash. He hung there for moments then said, "Run for it," and led off in a dash for the west side of the main-house. As with Hank, they got over there with no trouble. Fred did not stop to catch his breath, he pushed toward the southerly corner, removed his hat, got down low and looked around the rear of the house. Joe waited peering elsewhere, by all rights Hank should have been around here somewhere. Joe was thoroughly confused — and apprehensive. Nothing had gone right since they'd entered the yard, but back then by their calculations there should have been only Parsons and the Hawkin brothers. Then it turned out the way-station men were at the bunkhouse, which hiked the odds, an' now it appeared there were others out here neither Joe nor his companions had anticipated. Joe had been happy about being able to brace the Parsons place after nightfall. Right now he would have given ten dollars in new money for daylight.

The silence was nerve-wracking. Joe, unlike his companion, would have welcomed any kind of sound, even more gunfire.

Fred slipped around the back of the house. Joe followed him with the hair on the back of his neck standing straight up.

There was no one back there, nor were there light or sound inside the house. They got over near the rear door which hung open. Fred, who had grown leary of his companion, said, "I'll go in first. You wait; hide an' watch for anybody sneakin' around here."

Joe nodded as Fred reached the ajar door, eased it open a little more and stepped into pitch darkness which, in a way, was welcome and in another way was not. If there was a gunman in here, although he would be unable to see Fred any better'n Fred could see him, the gunman could be standing perfectly still and Fred had to move.

It was so dark, still and silent Fred could hear a clock ticking. He lifted out his Colt very carefully, placed a thumb pad over the hammer and moved as soundlessly as he could — until he stepped on a place in the floor where the wood squeaked. He moved swiftly to one side with his gun up and moving.

There was no gunshot. He used a soiled cuff to push sweat off his forehead and started moving again. He used up a full fifteen minutes making sure he was alone in the parlour, another fifteen minutes exploring elsewhere. He roused the dog who lived beneath the front veranda, but his barking was not very worried-sounding, nor should it have been; people commonly walked above his head.

The last room he entered was the kitchen, a rather large, cluttered room. He felt for the table that was usually in the centre of all ranch kitchens, found it and froze at a sound beyond the table.

The sound increased in intensity. Fred leathered his six-gun went around there and found Hank Lytle trussed like a turkey with a soiled rag tied firmly around his lower face.

The moment the gag was removed Hank's rush of words sounded run together. "I got inside . . . That's all I remember. Someone must have heard me comin' and was waiting beside the doorway . . . Fred, I got a thick skull. They tied me in here and went back to the parlour . . . I was comin' around when I heard a man cuss an' another man say, 'Parsons, you lyin' old bastard. How many more's out there?'" Hank paused as he got to his feet rubbing his wrists. "Parsons said he'd swear to gawd he didn't know who I was. The only men he knew besides himself an' the Hawkin boys, was the way-station crew. He said I wasn't none of them."

Hank leaned to kick the rope loose from his ankles as Fred said, "How many are there? We caught one over between the barn an' the bunk house. He had a federal lawman's badge in his pocket."

Hank straightened up quizzically scowling. "A U.S. Marshal? They didn't act like federal officers to me, Fred."

"How many was there?"

"Four. If they're lawmen of any kind I'll buy you a good horse."

Fred jerked his head, led the way

out back where Joe came from behind three stacked barrels. Fred gave Joe no time to ask questions, nor Hank time to answer any. He growled for them to follow, and went back around the house the way he had come. The hush was deeper than ever, not only in the yard but also in the night.

Hank asked where Charley was. All they could tell him was that Charley had gone looking for Hank, and that made Lytle frown with anxiety.

Fred hung fire until he thought the way was clear, then sprinted back to the bunkhouse, which was also empty with both doors hanging open. He led them to the north side of the building where he and Joe had left the unconscious stranger. The man was gone as were his plundered belongings which had been left in the dirt.

Joe was exasperated but Fred wasn't. He wished the man had still been there but was not surprised that he wasn't. His first blow had been hard enough, but it had taken the less strong strike to knock the stranger unconscious. He would not have still been there if he'd been struck down by the first blow. Too much time had passed.

Hank was worried about Charley. So was Fred as he led off in the direction of the barn. This time being extremely cautious, considerable time passed before they reached the spot where they had found the stranger. They still had a fair distance to cover and there was no decent cover, the barn, like most barns, was in an area by itself. There were corrals out back, but they offered no protection. Also, it was in the area where some of the shooting had occurred.

Fred went half way, then faded easterly toward the middle of the barn's long southern wall. There they flattened, listening and looking. As at the main-house, there was an almost unreal, deep stillness.

Fred motioned for Hank and Joe to wait, slipped west to the corner, got low and peered around. He saw nothing, even the corralled horses were dozing. He went back shaking his head. "No one, unless they're inside the barn bein' real quiet."

Without a word Joe turned easterly, went up as far as the corner, peered around with his gun in hand, then, to the surprise of both waiting men, Joe passed around to the front of the barn and was lost to sight. The tall Texan swore under his breath. If he ever went on another manhunt he was not going to do it if the cafeman was along.

But nothing happened. Joe eventually emerged from the rear barn opening, strolled around where his friends were facing the wrong direction and gave them both a bad start when he said, "No one's in there."

Another time Fred would have chewed on him up one side and down the other, but right now he cocked his head at a very faint sound of bootsteps coming out of the westerly darkness.

He made a guess about whoever

was approaching and swiftly took his companions up to the front of the barn and down inside where it was too dark to make out faces until they were very close, gestured for them to get on either side of the big doorless barn opening, which they did. All three of them could hear the oncoming man now, his stride was long and solid, whoever he was he had a definite destination in mind which the men from Cedar Bluff had no time to speculate about.

The man had a heavy step. Fred guessed he was large. Hank and Joe, on the opposite side of the opening made no judgements, they simply remained like statues with six-guns in their hands.

7

Under Suspicion

IT was a long wait, for while the man eventually did enter the barn, before that he caught a saddle animal in the corral, made a war-bridle of his rope, then led the animal toward the barn.

Inside, the men from Cedar Bluff were less tense. Tension was an emotion that was rarely self sustaining for long periods.

They got their next shock when the man halted just short of the barn opening and spoke, softly but distinctly, sounding disgruntled as he said, "Damned idiots."

He had the horse on a shank about eight feet to the rear when he entered the barn and in the utter silence heard a gun being cocked on his left side.

He halted stone-still. On the right side another gun was cocked.

The man, as Fred had guessed, was large. There were taller men but not very many as thick and broad. His immediate disadvantage was that his eyes were unaccustomed to the stygian darkness as Fred spoke.

"Drop your handgun!"

The gorilla-built silhouette faced in Fred's direction. Without haste he shucked his weapon. The others heard it fall. The man spoke quietly, sounding more disgruntled than ever. "Who the hell are you?"

No one answered. Fred gave another order. "Tie the horse to the stud ring. It's about ten feet in front of you on the barn upright. Move slow an' be extra careful. Move."

The man moved, but without extra haste. His eyes had still not become accustomed to pitch darkness. He found the pole, made the shank fast through a heavy steel ring embedded in the massive log upright, and turned.

He made out movement on both sides of the barn opening, but until the men from Cedar Bluff were close he could not distinguish faces nor outlines very well.

Fred considered their prisoner. None of them knew the man and he did not know them, but he broke the silence in a growly voice.

"Who are you fellers?"

The repeated question was ignored as it had been before. Fred was distinguishable, but barely, when he said, "It ain't who *we* are, Mister, it's who *you* are."

The thick man could finally make out faces, not in detail but well enough. Instead of answering Batson's question he said, "How many of them damned fools is there?"

"What damned fools, mister?"

"Outlaws like you fellers . . . Let me tell you somethin'. The army's convergin' from three directions. Personally, I don't give a damn what you do, but I'll give you some advice. Put down your weapons an get comfortable. If you make a run for it like your friends did, you'll meet up with soldiers, an' soldiers got a habit of shootin' on sight."

The men from Cedar Bluff gazed stone-facedly at their prisoner. Hank finally broke the silence. "Who do you think we are?" he asked.

The big, growly man peered at the harness-maker. "Damned highwaymen and renegades. We caught a bearded feller out by the coach. He told us you was part of the old man's organisation."

Hank started to argue but the skinny Texan cut him off with a gesture as he gave their prisoner an order. "Empty your pockets . . . If you got a hideout gun, don't try using it. Empty them!"

The thick man obeyed, slowly and clumsily. He had been in a foul mood before returning to the barn. What had happened since made his disagreeableness more pronounced. When his belongings were on the dirt barn floor Fred, who did not take his eyes off the large man, told Hank to sift through the personal effects, which Hank did.

During this interim the growly man spoke again. "Somethin' else you might want to ponder on; Your friends got about half the money off the stage an' run for it. You gents won't get a damned red cent, you dassn't try to run for it, an' military courts buy hang-rope by the bushel."

Hank grunted, arose and held out one hand palm up so his companions could see the little round badge with a star in the circle. Joe made an audible sigh. He was beginning to consider what had already occurred to him and Fred. Joe had a question. "Mister, have you got a friend with a lump on his head?"

The growly man nodded and stared at Joe. "Are you the feller who hit him?"

Joe did not reply, he instead put his attention upon the harness-maker, who answered the federal deputy marshal in his laconic way. "No, it wasn't him . . . You got a name, mister?"

"Alex Griffith. You got names?"

They gave him their names, then Fred launched into an explanation for their presence at the Parsons ranch, and lightly sketched in a few other things, such as the double-crossing old rogue at the Hawkin place. He did not mention the mean-faced old woman.

Marshal Griffith listened, leaned slowly to retrieve his six-gun and holster it. "If you're lyin' or tellin' the truth won't make much difference. The soldiers can sort that out." He turned his back to them to begin freeing his horse from the snubbing post. As he did this he almost indifferently said, "We got one of you, feller named Prentice." He faced around holding the slack lead-rope. "I got some ridin' to do, gents," he told them and walked to a saddle pole where he looped the rope and was about to rig out when Fred Batson went over, shoved the barrel of his cocked Colt into the lawman's back as he said, "You're not goin' anywhere. Leave the saddle on the ground and face around."

Marshal Griffith obeyed. His eyes narrowed slightly. He and the skinny tall man were less than twelve feet apart. Fred smiled into the more massive man's face. "Try it. Go right ahead."

Their unwavering stare remained locked on each other until Joe said, "For Chris'sake, Fred, knock him over the head an' let's get on with it."

Batson could have been deaf. He raised a stiff finger, placed it against the burly man's chest, and pushed. Instead of giving ground the massive man snarled at Fred. "The longer we stand here talkin', the farther them sons of bitches will get."

"You said the soldiers was all around."

"By my calculations, they got a long head-start. The army can't have got up here when this ruckus started."

Hank asked the prisoner how he and his friends happened to be inside the main-house, and got back a cryptic reply. "We approached from behind the main-house, got inside from out back an' would've got the drop if a danged dog under the porch hadn't commenced raising hell."

"The old man an' his friends caught you?"

"No. They were expectin' someone. Until it was too late for 'em to know we wasn't whoever they figured had arrived, we had 'em . . . But the old bastard fooled us. When I told him to shut up that danged dog, he said the dog only barked when friends of his was around . . . So we left three carbines fixed along the front winders, took the old goat an' his partners and would have got clear, but someone rose up from behind some barrels out back an' caught us redhanded . . . That feller one of you hit over the head was still inside when we marched the other three out of the house. When that

126

feller among the barrels rose up, one of my men went back, down the hall to the bedroom, shoved his weapon out an' cocked it. He was no more'n ten, twelve feet from that feller's back."

"So you trussed him an' left him in the kitchen. Well; do you recognise him, Mister Griffith?"

The dour large man jutted his jaw in Hank's direction. "Him," he answered as he leaned against the front of a tie-stall. He did not look even slightly intimidated as he studied his captors. "They're gettin' farther away," he said quietly, looking from face to face. "That ought to make you feel good — if you ever find them again, an' if they share what they took with 'em stuffed inside their shirts."

Once more Fred explained who they were and why they had been here. The big man seemed unimpressed. He was silent for a while before addressing them again. "Nice story, only the old man told us different."

Joe was tiring of this. "Tie him up

an' let's go find Charley."

Fred ignored the cafeman. He spoke to the big man. "Where's the stage coach?"

The big man made a tight, humourless smile. "Out in that deep arroyo where you fellers hid it." The big man also seemed to be tiring of this. Before he could speak again Fred asked how many companions he had out here. The big man raised three fingers of a ham-sized hand, and continued to regard the men from Cedar Bluff with a saturnine expression. "Three countin' me . . . If you got some idea of rescuin' your friend, go right ahead." His sour tight smile lingered. "But if I was you lads I'd saddle up an' high-tail it like your friends done."

Joe and Hank strolled to the rear barn opening and were surprised to see a pale, fish-belly sky. The night was almost finished. They could see a fair distance. The land was empty, they returned where Fred and the big man were and asked him where his friends were, if in fact he had companions.

The reply they got did not especially surprise them. "They went after the fellers who raided the money-box before we could get them." He shrugged powerful shoulders. "If they don't get 'em the army will . . . Gents, save yourselves some trouble, put your guns down an' get comfortable. It shouldn't be too long a wait."

Joe's curiosity prompted him to mention that single gunshot westerly, out where the arroyo was. The big man answered shortly. "When we come onto them one of 'em fired from horseback as they were leavin'."

"Which direction?"

"Northeast." The large man showed that death-head smile again. "If you ever see your friends again it'll be a cold day in hell. They're gone with as much money as they could pack, — an' you gents was left behind."

Hank answered that sharply. "You been told who we are an' what we're doin' down here."

129

"Sure," the large man said dryly. "That's why you hit a deputy U.S. Marshal over the head. That's why you fellers was tryin' to find your friends."

Joe had a sharp comment to make about that. "If we'd been lookin' for Parsons and the Hawkin brothers as part of their outfit, don't you figure we'd know right where to look? Mister we didn't know where that damned coach was until you told us."

Fred had formed an opinion about Deputy U.S. Marshall Griffith. He had figured everything out his way and nothing the men from Cedar Bluff could say would change his opinion. Fred jerked his head in the direction of the corrals out back. "Let's get saddled up."

Joe jutted his chin. "What about him?"

"Tie an' gag him, shove him into a stall an' forget him. Let's get a-horseback."

First, they tied Griffith, gagged him

130

and left him propped against the far wall of a stall. He did not say a word as they were doing this, but just before Hank fitted the lawman's own bandana into his mouth for a gag, he made another dour remark. "If you got a lick of sense, boys, you'll forget the money an' make a bee-line for Messico an' keep ridin' down there until you get lost."

They left the big man, went out back, brought animals inside to be rigged out, led the horses outside to be mounted and someone yelled from some distance westerly. Daylight was breaking. A man too distant for six-gun range was standing in plain view watching them. They left him standing there, jogged for a mile until the horses were 'warmed-out' then boosted them over into an easy lope with Fred and Hank out front. Hank had not wanted to leave before they found Charley but said nothing. As a hostage or just as a captive of lawmen, he would be safe enough.

They might even let him go; from the beginning of this manhunt Charley'd been worried about his wife back in town. The longer this took the more Charley would have worried.

They slackened to a steady walk with Fred watching the ground like a hunting dog. Last night, darkness had been their friend, the early morning was acting in the same way, they could read sign right up until they saw the north-south roadway, then one set of imprints veered southward. Someone had elected not to stay with the others. Fred made a shrewd guess. "The old man. Them Hawkin boys seem to work in tandem."

The tracks made a big sashay northward almost to within sight of the Cottonwood settlement before they began to bend around more southerly than easterly.

Fred made a little clucking sound, re-set his hat, got a cud settled in his cheek, spat once and rode with narrowed eyes and without haste.

After an hour of this, he drew rein in familiar territory and made a dry remark. "Told 'em to stay off her land, did she. Said she never wanted to see either of them again . . . " He raised a long arm. "The tracks is wheelin' around more southerly than easterly." He moved out, leaned to expectorate again, straightened in his saddle and gently shook his head.

"We know that miserable screwt she lives with would double-cross his own mother." Fred dropped his arm. "She didn't impress me too favourable either."

They followed the tracks for another mile or so then changed course, went a mile eastward, turned back angling a little southerly.

The sun was high and climbing before they reached one of the surrounding heights from which it was possible to look down into the ancient lake bed with its hundreds of round boulders.

A thin spindrift of smoke was rising from the stove pipe at the main-house.

Hank guessed someone had either partially closed the damper or was letting the breakfast fire die by itself.

They dismounted, tied their horses to spindly brush and went ahead on foot. They were functioning according to the harness-maker's hunch. So far, except for his initial big blunder over at the Parsons place he had done well enough to earn their respect.

They got belly-down and crawled to the edge of the easterly rim overlooking the old lake bed. Except for that spindly smoke there was no sign of life.

There were horses in a corral south of the barn. Hank squeezed his eyes almost closed but was unable to determine whether those were working animals or the horses of the men who had escaped back at the Parsons place. It was annoying not to be able to see if any of those animals were sweat darkened.

Joe considered his companions. They were beard-stubbled, rumpled with dark circles under their eyes. Joe assumed he looked no better, but it wasn't appearance that troubled him. He hadn't eaten since early the day before. His trade as a cafeman had ensured that he would never be hungry. The men beside him on the ground had not once mentioned food and as they lay now with their full interest on the area below, it appeared to Joe Angel nothing was farther from their thoughts than food and he was right.

Thirst would cause torment too, but not until the sun was directly overhead pouring its heat downward in this country of very little cover.

Fred was silent so long Joe finally spoke to break the hush. "They could have got over here, got fresh animals an' be gone."

That was a possibility, except for those tracks which, despite their sashaying, probably to confuse or slow pursuit, had ultimately led to the old lake bed.

They hadn't had enough time to be

very far if they'd been down there and left. The country along the mesa where the men from Cedar Bluff were lying, ran uninterrupted for many miles. In all that open country there were very few trees and none at all along the rims overlooking the ranch below. If the hunted men had left, there should be dust banners. Dust banners if they were many miles ahead, and if they were closer, they should have been visible to the men atop the *barranca*.

Joe hissed. Someone left the mainhouse, walked to the barn, disappeared inside and when the spies on the rim were preparing to rush back to chase a rider, the distant person emerged from the barn and began flinging seeds; about two dozen scrawny Mexican chickens appeared from nowhere. They ran, dashed, pecked each other and picked up grain as fast as they could.

Fred said, "The old woman."

They watched her return to the house, disappear inside as someone else came out, hitched his braces as he stood looking around, then trudged down to the barn. None of the watchers had difficulty identifying the raffish man who knew how to use a heliograph mirror.

He also disappeared inside the barn, and as before Joe got upset. "We better get back to the horses in case he rides off."

Fred did not move, he was squinting down there. Eventually, when the raffish man did not appear, Hank also got impatient.

Fred sensed their impatience. Without taking his eyes off the barn he said, "Not just yet."

His prescience was proven correct. The raffish man emerged from the barn, paused long enough to hitch at his braces, cast a slow gaze all around, then resume his march to the main-house.

8

Warm Trails

"WE got to sneak down there an' see if there's sweaty horses in the corral." As Fred made this remark he began pushing back from the rim until he could stand up, and that was when Hank spoke. "We left tracks an' there was the other tracks. If those U.S. Marshals don't track us down the army will. Fred . . . "

The skinny tall man looked solemnly at his companions when he interrupted Lytle. "If they track us, an' I expect they will, we still got maybe an hour . . . Gents, if the Hawkin boys aren't down there I'll eat my hat. If it was Parsons split off back by the road, it'll be up to the army to run him down."

138

They returned to the horses and began a long half-circle ride to reach the north part of the area far enough away not to be seen, then turned directly southward. Their horses were in better condition than their riders.

The heat was increasing, thirst became a problem as they led their animals toward the yard keeping the big barn between themselves and the main-house. Last night they could have done this better. Last night darkness had been their friend. This morning they were visible, not from the main-house but from just about every other direction.

They reached the yard, each man up front ready to clamp down if his horse scented other horses and would nicker.

They had a combination chicken yard and wagon shed between them and the barn. They left the horses tied there, went stealthily down the backside of the barn, still out of sight of the house, got inside where it was ten degrees cooler, and while Joe went searching for a trough of water, Fred and Hank stood just inside the rear barn opening where it was shadowy, and studied the horses in a nearby big round corral.

Two, a bay and a chestnut had marks made by sweaty saddleblankets, not quite dry but in warm morning sunlight they would be dry shortly.

Fred nodded without speaking. He had taken one hell of a gamble. Right now he was satisfied with himself. So far he had out-guessed everyone, and while a man's luck was as fickle as hell, he meant to push his luck to the limit.

Joe joined them wiping water from his chin. "The trough's half inside, half outside the farthest corral. The water's cold."

Hank pointed to the bay and chestnut. Joe pursed his lips to whistle, let his breath out instead. "They're in the house," he said quietly, and looked at the skinny tall man. "Time's runnin' out, Fred."

They went up to the front of the barn and peeked with only half their faces showing. Hank shook his head. The house wasn't much, planed wood badly weathered, a veranda that ran along the front, all of it at least thirty yards from the nearest ranch building. He wished this had been last night. The idea of crossing all that open yard had little appeal.

Graveyards had their share of heroes — and fools. Hank Lytle had no intention of being either.

Fred had a cud which he occasionally chewed as he stood like a stork pondering. Joe came back where Hank was. "Them people won't stay inside all day."

Fred turned. "We don't have all day."

His companions gazed at Fred. Joe asked a question. "We could ride off an' wait. The federal law or maybe the army'll be along. What do you think?"

"I think what I just told you — we

don't have all day. More'n likely we got maybe one hour."

Joe accepted that. "All right. Now tell me how we cross all that open yard without gettin' our heads blown off? An' tell me why we shouldn't let the marshals an' the army handle it from here on?"

Fred answered neither question, he returned to the front of the barn, stood a long time watching the house from inside, eventually turned again to address his companions.

"It ain't foolproof, gents, but I've seen it done. Each of us takes a horse, stays on the left side an' walk down the back of the barn, then straight toward the house."

Hank snorted. "It'd be a good idea — if horses was bulletproof, but they ain't. From in front of the house, at close range even a little derringer's slugs would go through any horse."

Fred returned to the front gloom with his back to his companions again. Restless Joe Angel strolled to the rear barn opening. It bothered hell out of him to be this close without being able to get any closer. He heard Hank say, "Maybe they'll be in the back of the house."

Fred replied without turning. "Maybe the old woman might be, but her boys'll be as jumpy as cats."

Joe returned from out back. "They know the law's on their trail, Fred. They know they got to ride. Sooner or later they got to come out an' get a-horseback. My guess is that they know they can't stay here much longer."

Fred continued to stand with his back to them watching the house. "It's time," he softly said. "If they don't come out soon we got to figure a way to get over there."

Hank also went up front to look out, but not so much at the house as at the yards of open space they would have to cross to reach the house.

Fred turned his head. "Maybe. Let's go open the corral gate. That'll keep em' inside. They'll hear the horses runnin'."

Joe came up to join the other two men. "They'll also know someone turned the horses loose," he said.

Fred shrugged. "We got to get over there an' we got to do it soon."

Hank put in his two-bits worth. "When they figure someone's out here, they'll fort up harder than ever."

Fred returned to watching the house, and Fred's companions watched Fred. His eagerness to reach the house seemed to be interfering with his judgment.

The Texan finally moved farther back in the barn, sat down and stared intently at his boots. Joe and Hank figured he was working out some way for the three of them to reach the house without getting killed, which he was, but the options were extremely limited — unless they were crazy enough to rush the house, in which case one of them might survive but as sure as hell's hot the others wouldn't.

He skived off a fresh sliver of molasses-cured, pocketed his clasp knife, settled the tobacco in his cheek and was about to speak when Joe hissed from up front. Someone was opening the front door over at the house. Hank and Fred went back up front. Fred spoke softly. "Good thing we didn't turn the horses loose."

The man who emerged was a disappointment, it was that raffish old screwt again, only this time he did not pause to snap his suspenders, he went to the edge of the porch and leaned on the railing looking far out.

Joe made a good guess. "He's lookin' for riders." Joe grinned a little. "Before the Hawkin boys come out."

Fred hoped mightily that this might be so. He and his companions were running out of time.

As they watched the man on the veranda Fred musingly said. "Gruber. I wonder how much they gave the old lady and him."

Neither of his companions answered,

they were watching the front of the house. It began to appear the man on the porch was never going to stop studying the countryside. He even spent several minutes peering along the rims closest to the house.

Hank said, "Sure as hell . . . " He did not finish but both Joe and Fred nodded. Gruber was taking a long time to assure himself there were no strangers within sight.

Eventually he turned, entered the house but left the door ajar. The distance was too great even on a clear, quiet day to hear anything being said over there. Hank went to the far side of the barn opening which allowed him to see the full length of the house. Fred got rid of his chew, cleared his pipes and got a disgusted look from Joe, not about what the Texan had done but because he made so much noise doing it.

Fred, still on the far north side of the opening softly said, "Well, well, well. It's the woman. She's coming over from the house."

Fred reacted swiftly. "Go out back to the north side of the barn," and led off walking fast. When they got around there he whispered his reason. "She'll be comin' to make sure there's no one around."

They heard her enter the barn, heard her moving erratically the way someone would do if they looked into stalls, into dark corners. She went out back where corralled horses gazed at her out of curiosity. They heard her go back inside and walk toward the yard. Fred let his breath out slowly. "Shouldn't be long now," he said quietly, jerked his head and led off back inside the barn.

He gestured toward horse-stalls. "Get in one. Hank, on the south side, Joe on the north side. I'll hide in the harness room."

His companions stared; the harness room would be exactly where the Hawkin brothers would go when they'd brought horses inside to be saddled and bridled. Joe was going to speak when

147

the clear sound of a door closing reached them. Joe had no opportunity to speak. Someone was coming from the house.

He ducked into the nearest horse stall, drew his handgun, crouched and waited. What he had been about to say was that if Fred was in the harness room, and both the Hawkin boys entered for their outfits, the odds were sure as hell not going to be in the Texan's favour.

They could not hear bootsteps, but they heard one man speak to another. "I sure hate to leave paw's stage."

The answer was roughly given. "The hell with paw an' his old coach. We should have done it all from horseback. If we had we'd be out of the territory by now. Wes, that's the last time you ever talk me into anything."

The voices came closer, only stopped when two men came in out of the yard. The gruff-voiced Hawkin growled at his brother. "Take that runnin' mare of maw's."

His brother was standing dead in his tracks. He probably did not hear his brother. He stood like stone for a moment, then very slowly began to twist as he looked around. He hissed at his brother, who was on his way to the harness room.

"Ambrose, look here."

The gruff man turned, gazed at his brother and went over where he was standing scowling at the ground. The gruff man also stood like stone as his brother spoke very softly. "Them ain't your boot tracks, an' they ain't mine nor maw's nor Harold's."

Joe and Hank began to shift noiselessly toward the front of their stalls. Fred was just inside the harness room next to the door with his six-gun in one hand at his side.

He could see the Hawkin boys through the long crack on the hinge-side of the door. They were like youngsters caught in some act they'd been warned about, they stood close as they slowly looked in all directions, slightly hunched, clearly tense.

Fred raised his handgun. When neither Hawkin boy spoke, the barn was as silent as a tomb. He had his thumbpad on the gnurled top of the Colt's hammer. He was beginning to draw the hammer back when a woman's harsh voice said, "I thought you'd be gone by now. You want to loaf until them lawmen arrive?"

Wes and Ambrose did not make a sound. The old woman sniffed disdainfully and walked past on her way to the corrals out back.

Her presence complicated things. As Fred listened from his harness room hideout he made some corrections — for one thing the old woman still hadn't sounded parent-like when she'd testily upbraided her sons. Another thing, there was no reason for the old woman to be here, unless female inquisitiveness had brought her to the barn to see if her sons had departed. Whatever the reason, Fred had his reasons for wanting to get this over with swiftly. He cocked his six-gun. When both of her sons craned around Fred stepped from the harness room doorway.

They stared, the gruff man told Fred to point his gun in a different direction, which had no effect upon the harness-maker. He told them to shuck their sidearms. As they were hesitating Hank rose up on one side and Joe appeared over a stall door on the other side.

Fred repeated it. "Shed them guns!"

Wes and Ambrose obeyed. As Fred moved away from the harness room doorway and halted with his back to the front opening, Hank and Joe came out of their stalls. They approached the area where Fred was facing the outlaws.

Joe, beyond reach of the outlaws, began to feel vindicated, Hank was also glad it was over. He had lost five pounds since leaving Cedar Bluff.

The three of them were facing their prisoners. Outside the sun was bearing down. Elsewhere, the raffish man suddenly appeared in the doorway.

He halted dead-still with his eyes wide and his mouth slack.

He was unarmed, in fact none of the men from Cedar Bluff had ever seen him wearing a weapon. They considered him an annoying interruption. Fred jerked his head for Gruber to get over where the other prisoners were standing. He asked if the raffish man carried a hide-out gun. Gruber shook his head, nevertheless Fred asked Hank to examine Gruber, which Hank did and afterwards straightened up shaking his head.

Hank also did something else. He was facing Fred whose back was to the front wide doorless opening. Hank nodded, stopped nodding with his eyes fixed on something behind Fred in the direction of the yard where a man's hard voice spoke quietly. "Put down the gun. All three of you, put 'em down!"

Fred froze. He had recognised that growly voice from over at the Parsons place. When the speaker did not get immediate obedience, he raised his voice slightly when he said, "All right, come in lads."

Two men entered from the rear barn opening. One had his hat perched atop a skimpy bandage.

The growly large man behind Fred lowered his voice as he tried one more time. "Put — the — guns — down. *Now!*"

Joe obeyed, Hank obeyed and Fred, facing both his friends, reluctantly lowered the hammer and let his six-gun drop.

The U.S. deputy marshal named Griffith holstered his sidearm, walked up behind Fred Batson, gazed at the others and poked Fred lightly in the back. "Turn around." Fred turned. He was half a head taller but nowhere nearly as thick as Griffith. When they were facing each other the federal lawman shook his head. "I told you . . . I told all of you . . . get a-horseback an' don't even look back."

Joe spoke sharply. "Yeah. Why? So's

you an' your friends could ride us down?"

Griffith's long upper lip lifted showing worn-even big white teeth. He eyed Joe briefly, then said, "We had a squad of blue-bellies with us. They left us where tracks showed someone split off goin' south . . . They'll catch him." The big man jerked his head. "Let's all of us go over to the house."

With no alternative they followed. Two men trailed in the rear with cocked Colts.

Up until now the only captive who had spoken was Joe, but when they reached the porch the big man faced them with thumbs hooked in his shellbelt. He stood a long time studying each face.

The old woman had overcome her surprise and fright. She lit into the big burly man with clenched fists at her side.

"Just who'n hell you think you are — you overgrown, hair-faced son of a bitch!"

154

Griffith reddened, but his gaze on the old woman, while not friendly, was not fierce either. It made a difference who called a man a son of a bitch. An old woman could get away with it — but it wasn't something even an old woman should do too often.

He showed her his badge, which she must have suspected he was carrying. She lit into him again. "Federal marshal's got no more right on my property than any other gawdamned trespasser . . . I'm goin' inside an' if you want to shoot an old woman in the back — you son of a bitch — do it!"

The deputy marshal with the bandaged head took two wide steps and blocked the doorway as his uninjured companion roughed up all the hostages pitching away not only guns but even clasp-knives.

Griffith waited until the old woman backed off then addressed Wes Hawkin. First he asked his name, after that he said, "Where's the money?" and locked his gaze on the other man.

Wes Hawkin was not the dour one. That was Ambrose. He spoke — before his brother could. "What money? You want to search us, maybe search the house? You better have a legal paper allowin' you to do it."

Griffith's hard gaze moved to Ambrose, whose stare never wavered. Griffith was silent so long it seemed he might not speak before he answered Ambrose Hawkin.

"We got all the legal rights we need, Mister Hawkin, an' I'm not goin' to stand out here and jawbone. Once more — an' if you want to stay healthy you'd better give the right answer. *Where is the army payroll?*"

The old woman flared up again, this time with fists on her hips as she glared at Marshal Griffith. "Search, you whiskered old goat. Go all over the place — look through the house, then the barn, an' don't forget the chicken house!"

Wes spoke before anyone else could.

"Maybe old man Parsons can help you, Marshal."

Griffith nodded but just barely. "Maybe. When they catch him." He had evidently made up his mind the hard one to deal with was dour Ambrose Hawkin, because he shifted his attention to him when next he spoke. "We're goin' to find it if we got to take your maw's buildings down a board at a time . . . We found the stage hid in that gully an' we found the money-box and some loose greenbacks where you'n that old man dropped 'em in your hurry to stuff your pockets an' maybe your shirts." Griffith paused. "Use your damned heads: We run you down, we found the coach an' the money box, an' we knew who stole the money, an' we got the money you fellers couldn't carry. All them things add up." Griffith paused again before also saying, "It's our job to catch thieves. The rest of it's up to the army. Did either of you boys ever watch a court martial?" Griffith's lips parted in a bleak smile.

157

"The army'll hang you. It won't be the first time . . . Now then, you want us to hand you over to the army, or do you want to help?"

Ambrose sneered. "Help you? So's you can get back the money an' then turn us over to the army?"

Griffith did not reply, but his bleak smile lingered. Hank thought he knew why. Ambrose's statement sounded as though he knew about the money, which was the only statement so far that hadn't been an outright denial of such knowledge.

9

Back In The Saddle

THE men from Cedar Bluff had been delegated a minor part in this affair. Marshal Griffith's full attention was on Ambrose and Wes Hawkin. Even the old woman's occasional outbursts did not distract him, and as for Gruber, he hovered near the kitchen door ignored by everyone.

One thing became clear as the palaver progressed; neither of the Hawkin boys were going to tell the marshal whatever they knew about the money, not even when he detailed everything beginning with the robbery up north, when and how it had been accomplished, down to their present predicament. He told them for about the eighth or tenth time he was going to find the money if someone had to die for it.

Hank and Joe had no doubt at all the deputy U.S. marshal meant exactly what he said. He hadn't threatened the Hawkin brothers, he had given them a promise.

The sun was well on its way, following the tracks of its million-year odyssey. Some corralled horses whinnied for their first bait of the day, and from a fair distance came the unsettling wail of coyotes on the prowl in a pack.

After asking one more question Marshal Griffith seemed ready to bow to the dogged intransigence of the Hawkin brothers. His final question was: "Ain't that one hell of a ride from the old man's place to here?"

Wes answered. Beside him Ambrose was regarding Marshal Griffith quizzically as his brother said, "It's a fair piece for a fact."

"We didn't find no place where you gents rested. All we found was where one of your trio cut loose an' headed south."

Wes answered that too. "Old man Parsons."

"Headin' for Messico, by any chance?" Griffith asked.

Ambrose was stone-silent, still regarding Griffith as though he had a suspicion but could not pin it down. For one thing, Griffith was being almost pleasant for a change. For another thing, everything he had said about the back-trail of the Hawkin boys had been correct, even to where and how they had camped.

If he had known so much weeks earlier, why hadn't he jumped the Hawkin boys after dark? Griffith was anything but dense, but right now he was projecting denseness and that bothered Ambrose.

The old woman went to her kitchen without anyone's permission, rattled a big old speckle-ware coffee pot, fired up the stove and set the pot to heat. She did all this without so much as looking out into the parlour.

One of Griffith's men took the

marshal aside to whisper. When the large man turned back he levelled a big, stiff finger. "One last chance," he told the Hawkin brothers, "Then we commence the search. If you don't want your maw's place turned inside out . . . *Where did the both of you cache the money you arrived over here with!*"

Ambrose stood like stone. Wes's eyes jumped around the room to only fleetingly meet the hard stare of the government deputy.

Wes, youngest and evidently least forceful of the brothers, took his cue from Ambrose and did not say a word.

But their mother did. She came storming out of the kitchen, eyes blazing. "You ransack this house," she told Marshal Griffith standing squarely in front of him, "An' I'll scalp you alive!"

Griffith looked stonily down into the upturned, angry face. He was expressionless. No one moved nor spoke. The old woman continued to stand so close to the marshal that they were almost touching, giving him look for look.

The skinny Texan's lips quirked as though he wanted to laugh. The woman was clearly old enough to be the mother of every man in the room. And while she was rawboned and sinewy she was not very tall. Griffith, on the other hand was twice as wide, twice as deep, and not the least bit intimidated as he answered her.

"We don't want to tear the place up, but we're here to recover the loot which is exactly what we figure to do." Griffith paused. "You could keep things like they are, just tell me what they done with the money they arrived here with."

For the first time, Fred, Hank and Joe began to suspect that for all her vituperation concerning her sons, right now she was not replying to the federal officer because she *did* know things. The question was, did she know about the stolen money; did she know where it was hidden?

Marshal Griffith allowed her plenty of time to agree to cooperate. When she stood there bleakly silent and hostile, Griffith raised his head, looked in the direction of his fellow deputy U.S. marshals and nodded.

They were turning away when Fred Batson dryly said, "Mister Griffith, you're takin' a long chance." He nodded to his companions plus the Hawkin boys and their fierce old mother. Griffith was unimpressed by the odds, he used his handgun to line them all up against the wall near the stone fireplace, then told his companions to begin their search.

Hank looked at Ambrose and Wes Hawkin. "They'll tear the place apart."

Neither man answered or for that matter paid any attention. They were watching Marshal Griffith.

The plundering deputy federal marshals made a racket yanking out drawers, dumping them, rummaging closets and chests, slamming doors open and closed. To Hank, Joe and Fred it sounded as though they were leaving no possible hiding place untouched.

The old woman's face was white, her eyes were squinted nearly closed. She had both hands knotted together beneath her apron.

Marshal Griffith stood like a statue, his eyes missing not even the slightest shift of weight among his lined-up hostages.

The noisy search continued from room to room. Finally the old woman turned and swung without aiming. Her fist, about the size of a small orange, caught Marshal Griffith in the chest. His free hand came up, caught her by the wrist and squeezed. She did not make a sound but her grimace spoke volumes; Griffith was a powerful man, her wrist was slight.

Neither of her sons said a word but Joe Angel did. "Let her go." When Griffith released the woman and shoved her back with the others Joe also said, "You incompetent danged fool — your money's gone north on a fast horse."

Everyone gazed at Joe. Only Fred Batson nodded. "Them lads of yours made enough noise to drown him out."

Griffith looked around. One hostage was missing — Gruber, who had been standing slightly apart from the others, closer to the kitchen door than to them, was no longer standing there.

Griffith bawled like a boar bear. When his deputies ran back to the parlour he was holstering his six-gun. "Mind this bunch! That shifty-eyed son of a bitch run for it. Mind 'em until I get back!"

The large man left the house by the front door moving faster than a man of his heft ordinarily would move. Inside, Fred Batson chuckled. No one heeded him but the deputy marshal with the bandaged head crossed to the open door to look down into the yard, leaving his companion to watch the hostages, which was not the wisest thing he ever did. As he was standing in the doorway peering down across the yard, waiting for the marshal to leave the barn and the yard in a dead run, the old woman fumbled in the drawer of a small table behind her, brought her right arm forward without haste and addressed the marshal who had been watching his companion over at the doorway.

What caught and held the attention of both deputy marshals was not the old woman, who normally would be harmless, but the weapon she was holding in both hands. It was a ten gauge shotgun that had been sawed off about ten or twelve inches from the stock. It wasn't simply a unique weapon, at close range it would be devastating. Even a man with a gun in his hand would be mincemeat before he could raise, cock and fire his weapon. The old woman had both hammers at full cock.

Her grouchy son smiled. The smile

became one of humour as he took a couple of steps toward the man in front, the one with the bandaged head.

The old woman swung the sawed-off shotgun quickly. "Get back," she told Ambrose. "Back against the wall!"

"Maw, we got to disarm . . . "

"Ambrose, I'd as leave blow your head off as look at you. *Get back!*"

In the period of shock that followed her vehemence, her eldest son retreated. Fred, who had been standing long enough, passed the nearest deputy marshal, took his handgun and went to lean on a chair as he cocked his six-gun in the direction of the man in the doorway. This deputy marshal's mother had not raised a hero, the deputy walked over near his companion, tossed his six-gun on a chair-seat and calmly considered the old woman, ignored Batson as he quietly said, "Ma'm, too much time's passed. Whether Mister Griffith catches that friend of yours or not, the army'll be along directly — then what? You figure to scare them off with that gun?"

The old woman ignored both the deputy and his words as she told Fred to make sure the man was completely disarmed, which Fred did as the old woman was turning toward her sons, still with the scattergun at full cock on both barrels.

The men from Cedar Bluff watched her. There was not a shred of motherly concern in her expression. On the contrary, she looked coldly contemptuous as she said, "I told you he couldn't be trusted."

Wes's retort resolved an issue which had once been paramount, but which had assumed less importance after the departure of Marshal Griffith. The fact that there *was* a cache.

"We was careful. Ambrose kept watch while I dug."

The old woman's sarcasm was biting. "Careful! I told you a hunnert times don't neither one of you have the brains of your paw. I warned you about

Harold being sneaky an' underhanded as a weasel. I'll lay you a hunnert to one if you go down there right now, all you'll find is a empty hole in the ground."

The old woman's venom carried over into other things she said, as when she ordered her sons to tie the pair of federal lawmen, and while they were obeying she asked if either Ambrose or Wes knew the men from Cedar Bluff. Both shook their heads without speaking, they were engrossed in lashing the federal deputies.

The woman turned her scattergun on Fred, Hank and Joe. "Who are you, an' don't lie to me this time."

"We're from Cedar Bluff. We lost our savings when your boys raided the bank."

The old woman accepted that. "Any more comin'?"

Fred shrugged. "I got no idea. Lady, how much money did your friend dig up and run with?"

She had a mouth like a bear trap.

She looked scornfully at the skinny tall Texan. "How would I know? They come in here on rode-down horses like the devil was chasin' 'em. Then you three come skulkin' around along with those lawmen. I never asked an' they never told me." She jerked her head. "Ask them."

Fred turned toward Ambrose and his brother. He knew which was the least likely to cooperate and which was not. He asked the old woman if she would object if he took Wes outside. She evidently did have some faint, lingering sense of maternal instinct because she said, "You don't go outside with no one."

The sound of a horse wheeling into the yard from the north provided brief distraction. One of the trussed men on the floor said, "Old lady, you'd better put that blunderbuss down. That'll be Mister Griffith, an' if he didn't find that feller who run off, he's not goin' to be in any mood for backin' off. He's got a hell of a temper."

171

The old woman put her fierce glare upon the speaker. "So have I. If he comes through that door even lookin' like trouble, I'll blow him in two."

For a moment there was silence before Fred faced Wes Hawkin. Batson was not especially menacing-looking, he was too skinny for that, but like most sinewy people he could move very fast.

He had a handful of Wes Hawkin's shirt before slamming the outlaw against the wall hard enough to rattle his teeth. Ambrose growled and moved. Hank stepped directly into his path. He did not wait, he swung high for the jaw and low for the soft parts. He missed the face strike but the second blow doubled Ambrose over. He was temporarily helpless. As he started to straighten, Joe Angel struck him on the right side of the head behind the ear. Ambrose went down and stayed down.

The old woman moved around until she could sluice all of them if she had to, but the beating of her eldest son seemed not to trouble her at all.

Fred held Wes pinned to the wall with a bony fist as he asked where, exactly, the cache had been. Wes answered in a breathless voice. "Under the manger of the last horse stall on the south side of the barn."

"How much was there?"

"I got no idea. We never had the time to count it. We just stuffed it into our shirts and run. I'd say we got maybe half of it."

Fred eased back, dropped his arm and was about to speak when someone rattled the front door. Did not open it, rattled it.

Everyone stared in that direction. When no one entered nor opened the door the old woman snarled at her youngest son. "Go see, Wesley."

The dour-looking man moved away from the wall, crossed to the door and had a hand on the latch string when a quiet voice spoke from somewhere in the vicinity of the kitchen.

"Lady, put that gun on the table . . . Lady, I'd as soon gut shoot you as look at you. *Put it on the table*!"

The men from Cedar Bluff held their breath. The old woman turned very slowly to face the kitchen doorway. Whoever was in there cocked a six-gun and spoke again, softly. "Three seconds, Lady. One, two . . . "

She put the scattergun on a table but did not move away from it. Hank, who did not like any of this, told her to move back away from the table, which she did without looking away from the kitchen doorway.

The man who came into the parlour looked tired, tucked-up and filthy. He gestured for the old woman to go to a chair and sit down. She obeyed that order too. The gunman turned, swept a glance at the stifling man on the floor before looking elsewhere. Hank, Joe and Fred looked relieved as Joe said, "Charley, we thought they'd caught you."

Charley Prentice said, "They did.

174

When they started north with the money box an' as much as was still in it, they herded me ahead, an' nothin' I could say made any difference ... You remember that way station north of Cottonwood? Well, that's where they left me with an In'ian woman. Then they rode back south. I could hear 'em."

Charley paused to consider his friends from Cedar Bluff. "You fellers look like something a tanyard pup would drag in ... Who's the feller on the floor?"

They identified Ambrose. They also identified the others. Charley asked about the money. They told him what had happened. He stood a long moment staring at Wes, shook his head and sank down in a chair near the pair of trussed lawmen. He ignored them as he addressed the harness-maker. "Fred, I thought I heard horsemen comin' this way from the south. If we get on our way back to town ... "

"We come for our money, Charley.

We'll go, but we got to find that scrawny old bastard who stole the money." Fred could still project his laconic humour. He said, "That danged money's been stole so many times it'll be wore thin before we find it."

They left the deputy marshals tied in the house on the floor, retied their weapons, and herded everyone else down to the barn where Fred and Hank sought, and found, the cache-hole Wes had described. As the old woman had predicted, it was empty.

The problem now was the old woman and her sons. They would not constitute much of a threat now that they were out-numbered and unarmed, but they could slow the pursuit.

As the old woman said, Harold Gruber would by now be so distant it was unlikely the pursuit would even see his dust.

Fred and Charley brought the horses from out back. Only two of them bore the old woman's mark. One of the horses the manhunters had acquired up in Cottonwood was missing. It was the horse Fred had ridden. They did not hunt for the animal; if it wasn't in the corral out back or in the barn, it had to be the animal Gruber had fled on.

While the men were working with their mounts the old woman ignored them all, even her sons, and garrulously complained about the man they were going after. "That man," she said, "was as worthless and sneaky as a coyote. He ate like a horse, never did a lick of work, and now has made all kinds of trouble."

Hank was rigging a horse when he spoke to her across the seat of his saddle, "Why did you put up with him?"

The old woman answered tartly. "Because he's my brother. Him'n me are all that's left of my family."

Fred had been puzzling over prisoners. He particularly did not like the idea of taking the old woman along, and he would have left her sons chained in the barn if he hadn't thought they

177

might get free before anyone returned for them. If he left her behind and chained her sons in the barn, she would turn them loose as sure as day followed night.

He rigged saddle animals in silence. Once, he glanced over at the old woman. She caught his look and snarled at him. "You're wastin' time, mister."

He replied tartly. "We'll be hard ridin' with precious few stops."

She sniffed. "I've been livin' hard and ridin' the same way since before you was born."

Fred led a horse over to her and held out the reins. She took them glaring at him.

When they were ready Wes and Ambrose were tied to their stirrups, the reins to the mounts were handed up to Joe and Charley.

The sun was still climbing when they left the yard at a walk, a gait they held to for about a mile before boosting their animals over into an easy, mile consuming lope.

10

The Trip Back

FOR the first time since they'd left Cedar Bluff Charley Prentice was willing to ride north. By this time he had heard most of the horror stories attendant on birthing.

When they finally reached the stage road there were many tracks going north, not all were fresh but there was enough crumbly soil to keep the man hunters astride.

The old woman did not say a word; her face was set in stone. Until Fred had a little time he remained out front but eventually he slackened until he was riding beside the old woman.

Tracking was difficult at the best of times, with shadows interfering it was hard to discern new sign from old, but the old woman scathingly remonstrated with her male companions as she pointed out their trail-wise errors of judgment as though each grown man had been a child.

Whatever attributes had contributed to the old woman's store of basic knowledge, she was for a fact the best tracker of them all.

She was also the person who brought up the subject of the stagecoach robbery and the lost payroll.

The old woman was queried about her brother. Mainly about why he had fled north instead of southward toward Mexico, the safe haven for all gringo outlaws.

She had no answer except to say her brother had once been jailed in Mexico and the experience had soured him deeply on all things having to do with Mexico.

Did he have friends in Cedar Bluff, or some town farther north? Not that she knew of. In fact, she told them, her brother rarely left her rock-pile ranch. He was not only underhanded and probably had a tape worm, but was also lazy. What riding had to be done, she had done.

Joe made a dry comment. "How'd you stand havin' anyone like that around?"

She threw a sulphurous look at the cafeman. "I told you — he's my brother."

Ambrose, being led along behind Joe, added his bit. "Danged poor reason for puttin' up with someone like him."

The old woman glared at her eldest son. "An' puttin' up with you — and your paw? At least Harold stayed around!"

The sun was shifting. The riders, with the possible exception of the old woman and her sullen sons, had neither rested nor eaten in a long time, which made it difficult for them to be alert. The Hawkin boys, especially the oldest one, recognised this and did not stop watching their captors. It would be next to impossible for them to escape with hands lashed behind them, boots tied to their stirrups and each animal being led, but they were desperate men. Neither doubted that if they were delivered to the law instead of the army, they would join their father in prison — or be hanged by the military authorities. If territorial law instead of civil law were invoked, they would hang, for while civil control had made strides west of the Missouri River, most of the country was still policed by the army, and would continue to be until territories became states and states were divided into counties which were incorporated civilian communities.

In the case of the Hawkin brothers it would probably be a toss-up. They hadn't just robbed a civilian bank, they had stolen an army payroll, an offence that ranked right up there with murder.

Fred, Hank, Joe and to some extent Charley Prentice, rode miles in pensive silence. Excepting sceptical Joe Angel, they believed they would get the bank's stolen funds back. They also believed the federal government would probably get nearly all its money back. They were tired men thinking wishful thoughts, all they really wanted was to reach Cedar Bluff, hand their prisoners over to Constable Talbot and let him worry about recovering the money and do whatever had to be done with the prisoners. They wanted to eat half a steer between the four of them, sleep for fifteen hours, maybe take an all-over bath after awakening even though it was a few days short of Saturday, and go over to the saloon.

They had passed through the Cottonwood settlement much earlier, had been astraddle a long time, most of it with heat adding to their weariness, and nothing was farther from their thoughts than the way-station miles behind them, the whiskered boss back yonder or the interruption during their meal when he and the Indian woman had exchanged remarks in some alien language.

It might not have mattered if they had

recalled that guttural exchange. They had long since begun to let-down, become less keyed-up and watchful. They only had another dozen miles or so to go before reaching town; they were no longer even concentrating on why they were riding north. Maybe they had come to accept the old woman's remark about never catching Harold Gruber. Even if they'd still been thinking of it, it would have been reasonable to assume they would dump that chore in Constable Talbot's lap too.

But regardless of tangents and tiredness, they were taken completely by surprise as they passed through a scanty stand of timber and a solitary rider appeared from the shadows on the east side, riding toward them looking affable until he drew rein about thirty feet away, drew and cocked a six-gun.

For ten seconds no one moved nor made a sound. Not until dour Ambrose Hawkin said, "What'n hell took you so long? I can dang near see the rooftops."

The stranger listened to Ambrose without taking his eyes off the men from Cedar Bluff, all armed, and by now all fully recovered and sitting straight in their saddles.

Wes's voice sounded strained as he said, "Austin, cut us loose."

The stranger acted deaf. He gestured with the cocked six-gun. "Get rid of your guns . . . careful now."

Joe obeyed first as he had done another time. He was not as fearful as he was thoroughly disgusted. So near — and yet so far!

The last man to disarm himself was Fred Batson, he had a cud in his cheek and expectorated first, then dropped his gun. The stranger looked longest at Fred, gestured toward him with the gun barrel and quietly said, "Get down, skinny. Cut your prisoners loose an' do it from my side." He also repeated his earlier warning. "Careful now."

Fred did not move. The stranger's gaze hardened on him. Hank could see a killing coming, swung off, dug out his clasp knife and without a glance at either the stranger or Batson, went over on the near side, slashed the wrist-binding of both prisoners, turned to face the gunman, who shifted his aimed gun to Hank. "Stirrups, too, friend."

The gunman was nondescript, his outfit was old and worn, his attire looked the same way. The man himself seemed calm, as well he could be being the one with the cocked gun. He needed a shave in a part of the country where about the only men who didn't were the ones who gave up shaving every morning and had beards.

He was watching Hank who had dug out the knife and was bending low to slash the bindings on Ambrose's stirrups, when hell broke loose.

Under the circumstances, with hot sunlight coming from overhead, dozing horses, and men whose attention was on the gunman or Hank, the gunshot was so unexpected the horses reacted faster than their riders. Joe's horse bucked him off on its second jump and fled toward Cedar Bluff. Hank and Fred fought to get their animals under control and succeeded, but Charley Prentice, with one fist locked around the horn, his other hand digging into cantle-leather was off on the right side. He was within moments of getting flung clear when Fred yanked his animal around, caught Charley by the scruff and pushed him back into the saddle.

There had been a second gunshot, but after the first one none of the men from Cedar Bluff nor their prisoners had time to consider that. Not until all but Joe, who stood in the roadway glaring after his disappearing horse swearing loudly, was making the only appreciable noise did Fred, Hank and Charley look to their left. The gunman's horse was racing westerly in a terrified belly-down run. His rider was lying on his back looking straight up without moving. He had shot his gun skyward as he had gone backwards off his horse, the instinctive jerk of a dying man.

The old woman was sitting the only horse who hadn't exploded. It was an old animal, grey around the eyes and muzzle. It had been startled enough to shy sideways but the old woman had anticipated this. She hadn't more than barely shifted in the saddle. Now, she was holding the reins in her left hand and a nickel-plated under-and-over .44 calibre derringer in her right hand, ignoring everything and every one except the man she had shot through the breastbone at a range within reach of her heavy, short-barrelled weapon of large bore.

Joe retrieved their weapons from the ground as he continued to swear.

Fred's attention was diverted as Ambrose and Wes picked up their reins for flight. He drew and aimed as he said, "Don't move. Neither of you. Set still and keep quiet . . . Hank, re-tie the sons of bitches." Fred paused facing the old woman who still had one slug left in her derringer. "Excuse me, Ma'm. Just a figure of speech."

If she heard him she gave no sign of it as she slowly returned the belly-gun to a pocket of her shapeless old coat.

While everyone but Joe Angel was recovering, the old woman addressed the man she had shot in a voice dripping with rancour. "You will lead my man into trouble then run out on him will you? I told him a hunnert times you wasn't to be trusted no farther than a man could throw a hawg — you son of a bitch!"

No one was shocked at her fierce vituperation but it made them curious. Fred asked who the gunman was — or had been. She finally looked away from the corpse, at Fred. "His name was Austin Camber. He talked my man into stealin' ten years back. I told him Austin Camber'd be the death of him. He told me to mind my own business, took the lads and rode off with Camber . . . I ain't felt as good in twenty years as I do right now."

189

She glared at her sons. "You boys wasn't born bad. For that you can thank your stupid paw — and that son of a bitch." Neither of her sons would meet her glare.

She watched the corpse being tied behind Charley Prentice's saddle, watched as her sons were re-tied, looked dispassionately at unhappy Joe Angel and finally growled at Fred. "You want to spend the night out, or get the lead out of your butt?" She threw in an aside to Joe without looking at him. "Get up behind me."

The cafeman looked from the old woman to the distant rooftops and declined. She snorted and squeezed her old horse.

Not a word passed for a couple of miles as all of them rode at a walk because of the cafeman being on foot, until Wes addressed his mother. "I remember when Paw give you that little gun one Christmas."

She did not turn as she replied. "It warn't Christmas, it was on my birthday. Onliest thing he ever give me 'ceptin' you two . . . Of the three I like the gun best."

Fred slackened a little, allowed the others to plod past as he reined in to ride stirrup with the old woman. He was slicing off a fresh cud when she spoke without looking at him. "Filthy habit, Mister Batson, always spittin', always got a cheek pouched out like a squirrel."

Fred didn't pouch the cud, he let it fall from the edge of his knife. They rode another fair distance before he quietly said. "This likely won't interest you. No reason it should. You're the only woman I ever knew who killed a man."

She finally faced him. "An' you think I should've give him a chance? Mister Batson, if I ever get a chance I'll bore you stiff with stories about Austin Camber." Her gaze was bitter. "You want to know what turned me away from preachers and churches? I've been to my share of burials and like to have thrown up when all them good words was said over rotten-bad people."

They rode in silence for another fair distance before Fred spoke again. "I grew up hard too, Miz Hawkin."

Her reply to that was quick and final. "Most folks did. Most folks didn't marry a weak-willed idiot who was a fine-lookin' man when he was young. Most folks didn't get their hearts squeezed empty when their only babies turned out bad as their father." She gazed at Fred, her eyes still bitter but for the first time showing something different, a pale shadow of interest.

He rode profiled to her, a tall man with a strong jaw. She sighed inwardly. Hell; he wasn't more'n maybe fifty. She was crowding sixty-six, and that was another hard blow to accept. Life was a gawdamned poor excuse for existing, better to be a bird than a two-legged critter. Maybe even a wild horse. Better to be anything but a female woman.

Gradually, a general conversation came about. The old woman took no part in it. Neither did her sons until Hank said, "We got to send back for the stage. There'll be money lyin' around back there."

Charley Prentice, uncomfortable with that sloshing-along dead man behind his cantle, had never in his life thought less of money. He growled at Hank. "Let the gawdamned army find their money. Maybe they can do that right."

"Our money," Hank retorted, and got back an answer he should have expected. "The hell with that too. I want to see my wife. To hell with everything else."

The old woman twisted in the saddle facing Charley, "How long you been married?" she asked.

Charley returned her look sourly. "Six years, an' now, finally we're expectin' our first."

The old woman rode a hundred yards before speaking again. "I birthed both my boys in a log cabin." She paused before speaking on. "Since then I've birthed maybe twenty, thirty young 'uns. Twins a couple of times. With twins you got to know what you're doin' an' be gawdawful careful." She sat forward again, and although those distant rooftops were more clearly visible now she seemed lost in her thoughts.

Charley interrupted her reverie. "How many did you lose?"

She twisted again, and glared. "None. Not a blessed one!"

Fred was still riding by her side. He had been gazing at distant rooftops too, right up until he had an idea. He spoke to the old woman in that quiet voice again. "When we get up yonder the lad there and I'd take it real kindly if you'd look at his wife — ma'm."

Her gaze, normally suspicious and unfriendly considered Fred for a moment. Of the entire lot including her bad seed he was the only one she cottoned to without making much of an effort to understand why. "I'd be glad to, Mister Batson."

He had another question for her.

194

"Along with birthin' children, maybe you've doctored horses?"

"An' mules, an' cattle, an' kids, dogs an' . . . Mister Batson?"

"I was wonderin', Miz Hawkin . . . It's none of my business . . . Cedar Bluff don't even have a midwife. Over the years we've lost young 'uns — an others. But you most likely don't care much for towns and folks . . . "

She stared straight at him. The shock of his suggestion did something Fred could not have anticipated; he had never married nor gotten to know women well. What he had done was open up something entirely new, fresh and something else — her husband had shunned people except others like himself; she had, up until the worst years of her marriage wanted to live in a town with people to see and talk to.

"Mister Batson, you got a hand-kerchief?"

He had one; he had been carrying it about a week. As he dug for it he

195

said, "It ain't exactly clean."

She flared at him. "Just give me the gawdamned thing."

He obeyed, looked sideways at her, eased his horse slightly ahead to cut off the sight of her from the others, and plodded along with his jaw set, wishing those damned rooftops up yonder weren't coming down to him so slowly.

He did do one thing he hadn't done for quite a few miles. While she was busy with the handkerchief he got out his plug, skived off a cud and cheeked it.

He rode stolidly, as the others were doing, all with their inner thoughts. Fred Batson's thoughts included having mentioned birthing kids and colts and whatnot, as well as mentioning living in a town. He could not understand why any such things would cause an emotional upheaval in an old woman.

He didn't bother to fathom it; most of his life, with the ugly parts, the good parts and the bad parts, he had learned acceptance. There was nothing he could do to change most of it, so he had decided to forget most of it. He was as direct and uncomplicated as most men of his time.

Joe was getting foot-sore. He used his legs and feet a lot at the cafe, but that was different. He had plodded along in daylong heat saying nothing of his increasing discomfort until he raised his head, saw something that put at least a small smidgen of hope in him as he raised an arm. "Dust. Someone's comin'."

The others tipped down hats and squinted eyes. It was more than 'someone' it looked like several riders and they were coming in a long lope.

Joe had something else to say. "I hope they got canteens. I been spittin' cotton the last few miles."

Fred left the old woman, rode up ahead, halted and shaded his eyes. "Hell of a bunch," he said. "Looks like maybe six or seven." He dropped his arm and turned toward his companions.

"If they're from town, gents . . . No lynchin'. I'd take it kindly if you'd stand with me about that."

Hank, Charley and Joe inclined their heads, but their concern was with the oncoming horsemen. If they were from town, and most likely they were, good; if they weren't from town — well — they'd just have to wait. As for their promise to Fred Batson, they had passed their words, but except for the mother of the outlaws, they might not have done so.

Fred too, thought of the old woman. About all she didn't need right now was to have to watch her outlaw sons hanged from trees. Whatever she had come to think of them — she had birthed them.

11

Return To Cedar Bluff

AN old man folks called 'Gunny' because he had been a Yankee artilleryman, dropped to a walk, rode with slack reins and gently shook his head.

There were six townsmen behind him. The four manhunters and the old woman halted in the centre of the road. Where the two parties came together no one said a word. The town posse-riders barred the roadway like statues.

Batson explained about the dead man behind Charley's cantle, explained about the old woman, and waited. Eventually a townsman with a high-pitched voice said. "Where is the money, Fred?"

Batson relaxed a little. "Scattered around the country. Some of it's out at a place owned by a man named

Parsons. Some of it's up yonder somewhere where a bean-bellied son of a bitch stole that dappled horse off me and run north with it."

The town liveryman sat like a stone. Several other townsmen eyed him askance. One posse-rider spoke bluntly. "That danged idiot rode straight into town an' the feller who owns that dappled horse caught him."

The silence settled. No names had been mentioned. Fred shifted uncomfortably in his saddle, shot a swift look in the old woman's direction, then spat and crossed both hands atop the saddlehorn as he looked at each posse-rider. He could guess what had happened. Harold Gruber, who hated Mexico, had fled north straight through Cedar Bluff into the arms of the owner of the dappled horse. Riding stolen horses was a hanging offence.

Fred said, "Well, gents?"

The liveryman considered the dead man and the old woman before he spoke. "Who's the feller ridin' double?"

The old man called 'Gunny' answered dryly. "His name's Camber. I knew him years back." The old man did not elaborate; his tone was gruffly unpleasant. There was probably a story behind his tenseness but for the moment identifying the corpse was all that mattered. Several of the posse-men knew the old woman by sight, but were now deliberately ignoring her. The two prisoners were of more interest. The man with the squeaky voice asked again about the money.

Fred searched him out. He had known the local banker for some years; he would have known that voice in the dark. He repeated what had been said before, but this time when he mentioned old Parsons a man who had been quiet previously, spoke.

"Yeah. He's been stealin' big unbranded calves as long as I've been in the territory."

No one took that up. Fred Batson had been forming a suspicion. He gazed at the liveryman, who was a stocky, hard-faced individual. "Where is the feller who was riding my grey horse?"

The silence stretched taut before the liveryman answered. "He was ridin' the horse I gave you, Fred."

Batson nodded in agreement and waited for the rest of it. "Well," the burly man said, "stealin' horses is a capital crime."

The old woman's gaze was fixed on the liveryman. He noticed and spat, wiped his mouth and seemed to be taking an inordinate length of time before speaking. He finally got it out in two words.

"Hung him." And before anyone else could speak he hurried the rest of it. "Fred, the town's fired up. Folks are mad . . . What could a man expect . . . Here comes this fat man ridin' a horse he had no right to be on, an' when we stopped him he bleated like a old ewe and commenced offerin' money around."

The speaker was disturbed enough

for it to be visible even in dying daylight. None of the other possemen spoke. Fred Batson avoided looking around at the old woman, they all did.

Batson gestured. "Let's go."

The banker bleated again. "What about the money?"

No one answered him. As important as the money was, there were other things more important; at least that's how they felt this evening. In the morning they might feel differently.

The old woman's face was masked by shadowy early dusk, but she rode straight up, her jaw toughset. Maybe, as she'd said, Harold Gruber was her brother, but possibly too she'd got pretty well fed up with him.

Cedar Bluff had lights showing almost the full length of town. A rider loped ahead. When the drooping manhunters came in from the south some bull-bass voiced individual up near the saloon hollered riders were coming from south of town which brought folks out from all directions. Charley Prentice peeled off in a lope, ignored shouts as he went past and flung off out front of his hotel, didn't even bother to loop his reins and hurried inside.

Fred watched the plankwalks. Normally this time of day people would have been at supper. It seemed to him that everyone was lining the plankwalks. They were noisy right up until they saw Charley hasten past with that flopping dead man behind his saddle, then silence settled.

Several of the town-riders including the banker left the others out front of the livery barn where the proprietor went down the runway, dragged an old chair into place, climbed on it, lighted the lantern, climbed down and shoved the chair aside as men came inside leading horses.

Constable Talbot, who hadn't been with the townriders, came down the runway looking sour. He asked who that was behind Charley's saddle and did not receive an answer from dog-tired men. He turned angry and repeated the question. Foot-sore Joe Angel faded away in the direction of his cafe. Hank Lytle the blacksmith straightened up as he said, "Ask the lady," and bent down again to free his latigo.

Talbot turned. He knew her by sight. "Who was he?"

She replied in a dead-calm voice. "Austin Camber. You ever heard of him?"

Constable Talbot regarded her in glowering silence. She turned her back on him. For a moment Fred thought the lawman was going to light into her, and waited. When Talbot eventually faced in a different direction Fred went back to off-saddling and Constable Talbot approached the town blacksmith. "Hank."

"Yeah."

"We're shy two hundred and eleven dollars."

"Off the fat feller . . . What was his name?"

"Gruber."

"Why tell me, Mister Talbot?"

"Because I was told someone seen you take some of the money he was spillin' all over the place before we hung him."

"Did you now?" the blacksmith said straightening around to face the town constable, clearly indignant. "Whoever told you that is a danged liar. I wasn't nowhere near when he got hung, an' that's a danged fact."

For a moment they faced each other before Constable Talbot did as he had done with the old woman, he turned his attention elsewhere.

The liveryman had not said a word since they'd entered his runway. Night was down, finally, the old woman finished caring for her horse. Fred Batson was prolonging small details until she was finished, then said, "Miz Hawkin, I'll take you up to the roomin' house."

As they were leaving Constable Talbot told the old woman not to attempt to leave Cedar Bluff. She did not say a word, she turned, stared at the waspish lawman, grunted and left the livery barn beside tall, skinny Fred Batson.

The moment she was gone Constable Talbot lit into her sons. Wes was the less forceful of the two so the threatening lawman had little trouble with him but Ambrose was tougher. He gave as good as he got. When Talbot was angry enough to strike the man whose arms were bound, the liveryman growled at him. "I'll untie him, Mister Talbot. Even a dog deserves a chance."

Nothing came of this backing and filling, nor had the liveryman expected it to. He, as well as most other residents of Cedar Bluff, knew their town constable. He wasn't exactly a bully but he came very close to being one. Right now, what particularly annoyed him was the fact that four townsmen had done what he had been unable to do.

When Fred and the old woman entered the hotel there was a commotion in the rear of the establishment, male roomers were milling like bewildered chickens. When they saw Fred and the old woman they rushed forward, all talking at once. One man, squatty, bull-like whose head and neck were the same size, took the old woman's arm in a hard grip. "Lydia," he exclaimed. "Thank gawd. We didn't know what to do an' Charley's about to go out of his head."

The old woman jerked free and glared. "What's the matter with you, Will Clements? Leave go of me."

The bull-necked man released his grip but still blocked the hallway. "It's Charley's wife, she's havin' a baby. It's not comin' right. She's weaker'n a kitten. We tried to find someone who knew what to do."

The old woman scowled at the bull-necked man, "Where is she?"

The bull-necked man reached to pull her along. She jerked away, "I ain't

208

blind. Just lead the way . . . Just you, Will. The rest of you go on about business. Go along. Git!"

Fred Batson trailed the old woman and the agitated man named Clements. The bedroom was large and better furnished than any other room. There was a popping iron stove that made the room insufferably hot. The old woman stopped, looked around, ignored Charley, went to the stove, slanted the damper to lessen the heat, opened a window, went to a large crockery bowl which she filled with water as she gave orders. "Mister Prentice, get out of here. Go in the kitchen, drink some coffee. I'll call you. Don't argue; we don't have that much time. Mr Batson, you stay. Clear out the rest of you, an' stay out."

Charley, who was frantic, had to be pushed out of the room by Fred Batson. He beat on the door from outside but Fred barred it from inside.

The old woman had her sleeves rolled. She had shed her coat when she leaned over the heavily perspiring younger woman. Her voice did not sound at all as it had before as she asked questions.

Fred was fascinated. He'd never seen a human birthing before, nor had he expected the old woman to be so different when she began her examination. She spoke in a low tone, speaking to herself as she said, "Hung up. An' there's somethin' else." In a louder tone she told Fred to re-fill the bowl and put it where she could reach it.

Her back barred Fred's vision from over by the door but her movements indicated that what she had told him about birthing had been gospel truth. Fred, who knew nothing of such things, nevertheless knew experienced professionalism when he saw it.

Charley's wife was a pale, sweaty, weak woman, at times incoherent, at other times lucid enough to whimper. The old woman told her to strain, she repeated it several times but either the younger woman was too weak for the effort or did not understand.

Fred watched the midwife straighten up, wipe her brow with a towel and stand indecisively for a moment before she leaned, using gentle but persistent force, allowing moments to pass before repeating the process. Both women were sweating now. Fred sensed that something was wrong.

Then the baby arrived.

It feebly struggled until it was raised by the ankles and slapped twice. The noise it made sounded very loud for such a small creature. The old woman turned. "Take it," she told Fred. "No, not wrong side up. Wrap it in something, use one of those towels. Cradle it in your arms. Oh for gawd's sake didn't you ever hold a baby? Like this — now dry it and cradle it."

The old woman turned back and gasped. "That's what it was. Son of a bitch!" She huddled over Charley's wife. Fred was fully occupied with the baby, didn't hear the old woman alternately praying and swearing as she repeated her pressuring and relaxing.

She became silent with desperation.

Fred's baby had the lungs of a horse, the men in the kitchen could hear its bellowing. Several of them had been through this and congratulated Prentice. His reaction to the screams was different. He sprang from his chair and rushed down the hall to beat on the barred door. When he was bawling his loudest the old woman slapped the second pair of buttocks. The result was predictable, the second child let go with a racket that drowned out its father's noise.

One of the men in the hallway with Charley said, "By gawd, you got twins!"

Charley stared at the man, stunned into silence, went to a chair and sat down. There was no mistaking it, the howling coming from the birthing room was being made by two babies, not the one he and his wife had planned for all the months of waiting.

Two men left the hotel to spread the news. To anyone's knowledge there had never been a set of twins birthed in Cedar Bluff.

The old woman handed Fred the second baby almost indifferently and went to work on the mother, who looked to Fred more dead than alive.

Fred used the last towel. The squalling, erratically moving and jerking babies kept him fully occupied. Ten couldn't have kept him busier. He had no time to look in the direction of the bed but he heard the old woman say, "Merciful God," twice, as she worked. She blocked Fred's view, which he wouldn't have had time for anyway.

The hotel was silent everywhere except in the birthing room. Someone had brought two bottles from the saloon, the men were sitting comfortably in the parlour passing the bottles around. Twins for gawd's sake!

Charley had one drink and refused more. He was still stunned. He did what might have been expected in his condition. He passed out from exhaustion.

The old woman stood over the birthing bed and during a lull in the caterwauling asked Fred what the woman's name was.

"Lydia Prentice. That's her husband who . . . "

"I know who her husband is, Mister Batson. Are you sure that's her name?"

"I'm sure. I've known them since they came here."

"Well; that's my name too. Lydia. I haven't heard of no one with my name in more years'n you are old."

"How is she . . . Lydia?"

"It's the bleeding. I'm waitin' it out. It seems to be lettin' up, but she'll be abed for a month, little mite of a thing." The inevitable bitterness arrived. "Men! They don't figure what this does to a woman. They don't figure at all, and when the birthin' comes they go out'n get drunk to celebrate."

Fred stole a moment to go stand

beside the old woman. For a fact Charley's wife seemed to be scarcely breathing. When he commented on this the old woman gave a sharp reply. "This here's the only time her breathin' has been normal since gawd knows when." She was prepared to say more, to say that a man who'd rush off after outlaws with his wife in this condition ought to be horse-whipped.

Fred returned to the babies.

The old woman sank down in a chair, she looked drawn to the point of collapse but she did not take her eyes off Charley's wife.

Someone timidly knocked on the door. The old woman called a challenge. It was Charley, puffy-eyed, grey-faced, half sick from all he'd endured for the past few days. He asked how his wife was.

The old woman jutted her chin in the direction of the twins. "You got two fine baby boys. Your wife'll come along — but real slow. When she's able to be up an around don't let her do no heavy liftin', no hard work for at least a month unless you want to kill her."

Charley went to the bed, knelt, wiped his wife's sweaty forehead and kissed her. She barely stirred, did not open her eyes, Charley leaned back, stared intently and without turning asked the old woman if his wife was going to die. His voice was barely audible.

Lydia Hawkin heaved tiredly out of the chair, crossed to bedside, stood a moment watching the sleeping woman, and did what Fred thought was a surprising thing, she gently put a rough hand on Charley's shoulder and let it rest there as she said, "I've never lost one. She'll live — but it's goin' to be a while. Now go get some sleep, you look like warmed-over death. Go on. If there's a problem I'll come get you."

She eased Charley to his feet and guided him carefully from the room. As she closed and barred the door she leaned on it gazing at the babies. Fred couldn't quiet them but he had them clean and wrapped.

The old woman said, "I like that in a man, Mister Batson." At Fred's mildly baffled look she shoved off the door and crossed to where the babies were sleepily whimpering. One had the hiccups. He asked what it was the old woman liked and she replied while leaning to examine the babies.

"He looked over here, but he went straight to his wife." She looked up. "You should have got married, Mister Batson." She said no more, returned to her chair, sank heavily down and within five minutes she was sound asleep.

Fred also sought a chair. For the time being the babies were quiet. He had an idea that would not last but closed his eyes anyway. He was right, but at least he got a couple of hours of badly-needed rest.

12

End Of The Trail

CONSTABLE Talbot's mood had only marginally improved by the following morning when a dusty, rumpled troop of cavalry arrived in Cedar Bluff, which caused quick interest — and consternation. They had taken down the man they had hanged as a horsethief but he was not buried, he was in a pine box set upon two sawhorses in the carpenter's shop. It was the worried carpenter who came looking for the constable at the cafe, told him soldiers were in town and scuttled back to his shop to cover the pine box with blankets.

Talbot crossed to the livery barn where the soldiers were putting up their animals, found a tight-lipped captain conversing with a stone-faced liveryman, and had to wait.

There hadn't been what looked to Constable Talbot like an entire company of soldiers in Cedar Bluff since he could remember. While watching and waiting, Constable Talbot took the measure of the thin-lipped officer. He carried no surplus flesh, was greying at the temples and had the expression of an officer who unquestionably obeyed orders.

It was a good guess, when the captain, whose name was Arthur Hamilton, detached himself from his supervisory duties, leaving them to a grizzled older man, a senior sergeant, John Talbot introduced himself and asked if the soldiers had found the stolen payroll.

Captain Hamilton, clearly a 'lifer' with a career officer's opinion of civilian lawmen, removed his gauntlets and tucked them under his belt before replying, "We found all but sixteen dollars, Mister Talbot. We also caught an old rascal named Parsons who helped hatch the robbery scheme and several others. They are on their way southeast to Fort Stanhope to be tried by a court martial." The captain regarded Constable Talbot with a flinty gaze. "The reason we came up here this morning is to find two men named Hawkin. We've rounded up all the others that we know of. They're on their way to Stanhope too. Mister Talbot, do you have any prisoners who could have been connected with the robbery?"

John Talbot was intimidated by the steely-eyed officer whose words seemed to be carefully selected and delivered in a voice lacking inflection. "I got two. The Hawkin boys."

"I'll give you a receipt for them, Mister Talbot." The captain was briefly diverted by some grumbling comment by the grizzled sergeant. He nodded and faced John Talbot again. "I know your bank was robbed. Possibly some of the money we recovered came from your bank. But my orders were to find the payroll and bring it back. If some of the money we recovered came from your bank, you'll have to take that up with the adjutant general's office in Washington. The money we recovered is in my view army property."

Talbot nodded understanding. He was to get an education in army procedures; adjutant generals were unyielding individuals. Since all greenbacks looked alike, it would be required of the constable that he provide proof part of the recovered loot had come from the local bank, an impossible thing to prove.

He took the officer and two soldiers to the jailhouse, and got a surprise. Ambrose Hawkin was standing over his brother who was mumbling incoherently on a cot, covered with sweat. He had a raging fever.

The stony-faced officer stood over the bunk in silence. Ambrose was worried and antagonistic. When the officer asked if he could travel, Ambrose stared at him, then gestured. "He don't know where he is. He'd never make it to the end of town. Mister, if you move him, you'll sure as hell kill him."

The officer continued to regard Wes Hawkin. "When did he come down with this?"

Ambrose answered harshly. "Some time in the night. I hollered myself hoarse. Couldn't raise a soul." Ambrose glared at Constable Talbot. "If he dies I'm goin' to hold you responsible."

The captain walked out of the cell without another word. Back in the office he made his decision. His orders were to recover the payroll and return with it as quickly as possible. He said, "Mister Talbot, I'm going to leave him in your custody. When he's able to be moved send word to Fort Stanhope and I'll send troopers for him. Now, my men and I haven't eaten. We'll pick up the other prisoner later. Excuse me."

After the soldiers left John Talbot returned to his cell room. Ambrose Hawkin met him with the bars between them, he was in a red-faced fury. He swore at the constable and gripped the steel bars until his knuckles were white. Talbot did not enter the cell, he returned to his office, sat down and stared at the wall. From the appearance of the younger Hawkin he was going to die. Talbot groaned.

It was mid-day before the soldiers left town, fed, their animals fed and rested, for the long ride to Fort Stanhope. Fred Batson heard of what had happened from the constable. He went to see for himself. The younger Hawkin was sweat-soaked and only rarely coherent. Fred returned to the office with John Talbot, listened to what the constable had to say about recovering the bank's money, and went up to the hotel to tell the old woman of her son's condition, and got a surprise. She showed only minimal concern as she said, "He gets it every now an' then. Swamp fever. He's had it since he was a lad. It comes on him, he gets out of his head. I keep medicine for him. Will you take me down there?"

Fred agreed, but stood in thought for a moment, then asked if the fever lasted. The old woman's reply reinforced Batson's suspicion. "Three, four days."

"Without the medicine?"

"Maybe six, seven days."

"Could he die from it?"

"He hasn't yet an' he's had it for a long time."

"Suppose we wait until this evening when the constable's havin' supper before we go down there."

She looked at him. "You got somethin' in mind?"

Instead of answering the question Batson asked one of his own. "The army took Ambrose. Would you say you favour your youngest?"

"I always favoured him. What set me against him was he'd never listen to me. He'd only listen to his paw and his brother. I've cried a barrel full of tears over that. Wes is too easy led. He's always been."

Fred smiled a little at the old woman.

"After you dose him with the medicine how long before he can set a horse?"

The old woman stared without blinking. She did not answer the question, instead she said, "How can you do it? Why would you?"

Fred's reply was thoughtful. "He's all you got left. If the medicine'll work in a couple of days . . . "

She arose from her chair. "How . . . ?"

"When Talbot's at supper — if Wes can ride."

"And me?"

"Go with him."

The old woman considered. She did not like leaving Charley Prentice's wife with two babies she was too weak to care for. She did not want to lose her only son, either. "Can you find a woman to look after the babies and their mother?"

Fred was confident he could so he nodded. "I'll be back when I see the constable headin' for the cafe."

It was dusk when they went down the back alley, the old woman doused her son with a bitter white powder, they slipped back the way they had come. They repeated this process the next night. The third day Fred visited the jailhouse. Constable Talbot told him young Hawkin was weak as a kitten but pretty well over his fever.

At midnight the old woman and Fred returned to the jailhouse, freed her youngest son and went with Fred to a corral of loose horses, selected two, rigged them out and were ready to ride when the old woman went up to Fred, gripped his shoulders and kissed him squarely on the mouth.

He stood out back in the darkness until he could no longer hear them. They had a long head-start before the owner of the horses missed them. By the time he could dragoon riders to go in pursuit they were even farther away and still riding. They were never heard of again. Neither were letters to the adjutant general's office in Washington. Neither was John Talbot who was fired as town constable after the escape of young Hawkin. It had been a long, arduous trail, full of twists and tangents. The bank's depositors lost some of their money but they had stories to tell for the rest of their lives.

THE END

TOP HAND
Wade Everett

The Broken T was big. But no ranch is big enough to let a man hide from himself.

GUN WOLVES OF LOBO BASIN
Lee Floren

The Feud was a blood debt. When Smoke Talbot found the outlaws who gunned down his folks he aimed to nail their hide to the barn door.

SHOTGUN SHARKEY
Marshall Grover

The westbound coach carrying the indomitable Larry and Stretch headed for a shooting showdown.

FIGHTING RAMROD
Charles N. Heckelmann

Most men would have cut their losses, but Frazer counted the bullets in his guns and said he'd soak the range in blood before he'd give up another inch of what was his.

LONE GUN
Eric Allen

Smoke Blackbird had been away too long. The Lequires had seized the Blackbird farm, forcing the Indians and settlers off, and no one seemed willing to fight! He had to fight alone.

THE THIRD RIDER
Barry Cord

Mel Rawlins wasn't going to let anything stand in his way. His father was murdered, his two brothers gone. Now Mel rode for vengeance.

FARGO: MASSACRE RIVER
John Benteen

The ambushers up ahead had now blocked the road. Fargo's convoy was a jumble, a perfect target for the insurgents' weapons!

SUNDANCE: DEATH IN THE LAVA
John Benteen

The Modoc's captured the wagon train and its cargo of gold. But now the halfbreed they called Sundance was going after it . . .

HARSH RECKONING
Phil Ketchum

Five years of keeping himself alive in a brutal prison had made Brand tough and careless about who he gunned down . . .

BRETT RANDALL, GAMBLER
E. B. Mann

Larry Day had the choice of running away from the law or of assuming a dead man's place. No matter what he decided he was bound to end up dead.

THE GUNSHARP
William R. Cox

The Eggerleys weren't very smart. They trained their sights on Will Carney and Arizona's biggest blood bath began.

THE DEPUTY OF SAN RIANO
Lawrence A. Keating and
Al. P. Nelson

When a man fell dead from his horse, Ed Grant was spotted riding away from the scene. The deputy sheriff rode out after him and came up against everything from gunfire to dynamite.

HELL RIDERS
Steve Mensing

Wade Walker's kid brother, Duane, was locked up in the Silver City jail facing a rope at dawn. Wade was a ruthless outlaw, but he was smart, and he had vowed to have his brother out of jail before morning!

DESERT OF THE DAMNED
Nelson Nye

The law was after him for the murder of a marshal — a murder he didn't commit. Breen was after him for revenge — and Breen wouldn't stop at anything . . . blackmail, a frameup . . . or murder.

DAY OF THE COMANCHEROS
Steven C. Lawrence

Their very name struck terror into men's hearts — the Comancheros, a savage army of cutthroats who swept across Texas, leaving behind a bloodstained trail of robbery and murder.

FARGO: PANAMA GOLD
John Benteen

With foreign money behind him, Buckner was going to destroy the Panama Canal before it could be completed. Fargo's job was to stop Buckner.

FARGO:
THE SHARPSHOOTERS
John Benteen

The Canfield clan, thirty strong were raising hell in Texas. Fargo was tough enough to hold his own against the whole clan.

PISTOL LAW
Paul Evan Lehman

Lance Jones came back to Mustang for just one thing — revenge! Revenge on the people who had him thrown in jail.

ARIZONA DRIFTERS
W. C. Tuttle

When drifting Dutton and Lonnie Steelman decide to become partners they find that they have a common enemy in the formidable Thurston brothers.

TOMBSTONE
Matt Braun

Wells Fargo paid Luke Starbuck to outgun the silver-thieving stagecoach gang at Tombstone. Before long Luke can see the only thing bearing fruit in this eldorado will be the gallows tree.

HIGH BORDER RIDERS
Lee Floren

Buckshot McKee and Tortilla Joe cut the trail of a border tough who was running Mexican beef into Texas. They stopped the smuggler in his tracks.